THE
Fitzy Resolution

A. D. DeSena

Cover: Bill Bergin   Edited by Paul J. DeSena

I would like to thank my family, friends, and wife.
I would especially like to thank Bill Bergin, Paul DeSena, and Bryan Emerson.
This book is dedicated to the memory of Casey Lee.

PROLOGUE

The world of dogs has been obscure despite the fact that they live in plain sight of their human counterparts. The following story reflects my efforts in piecing together various canine historical documents over a period of many years. Occasionally, there are certain canine words that have no direct translation and can only be approximated by a phrase or a description. These words can only be translated to their human English phonetic equivalent because the actual pronunciation would be impossible to translate. Though dogs communicate through barks, growls, whimpers, and whines in much the same way that humans speak, they can do so on frequencies that humans cannot hear. They also communicate through body language and their famous scentimas, which are layered particles that are separated in time but which together can comprise a complex phrase, sentence, or even intonation. Only canines can fully observe and understand these types of communication, but I have nevertheless attempted to be as faithful as possible in relating them. This translation marks the onset of a drastic change in the socio-political climate of the canines and is offered as an explanation of recent events. Any storyline involved with the events is purely guesswork, intended to bridge the known content of confirmed events.

MEETING

Casey shook herself with a hint of anxiety. She was late for the meeting, but only by a few hours. Since canine schedules were yoked to the whims of humans, dogs differentiated little between gaps of time in minutes or hours despite their shorter lifespan. The other committee dogs would surely not be concerned with what was considered to be a brief delay. Casey mentally prepared herself for the agenda. She was the head of the Committee of Inter-Canine Communication, and though the length of the agenda annoyed her tremendously, it might mean her committee was gaining in importance. She was only a junior senator, but the committee was entrusted to her because of her sweeping popularity. In reality, her position was not especially prestigious, certainly not so much so as any of the coveted positions on the Committee for Human Endearment or even the Committee of Canine Health. Despite that, the agenda was long today, and any of the issues addressed could mean more responsibility down the line.

Casey was a yellow Labrador Retriever of three years of age. Husky in body habitus by any standards, her fat tail reflected a healthy appetite and abundant food. Her coat was white in spots, and she had a notable white crescent on her chest in contrast to her light tan fur around it. Her floppy ears were a dark tan, and they highlighted her face, a shade of tan lighter, and her hazel eyes.

It was a cool summer day with warm, but not oppressive sunshine, and the neighborhood lay spread before her. It was perfect weather for mild exertion that would not lead to panting. Casey's eyes drank in the view before getting to business. Human homes were set back, maybe two to three hundred feet from the street and appeared to spit out their homogenous green lawns. Those same lawns rippled casually from a touch of wind, but, if one were to look closely, one would see that the edges of the grass near the streets remained as still as a statue. Heavy with information, innuendo, and other particulars, the edges of the lawns of this neighborhood contained official canine governmental scentimas.

As Casey walked on the way to the meeting, she sniffed, and the scentimas laid down by the various other committee members and other senators came to her like pages flipped rapid-fire in a book. Had it not been for the scentimas, the canine civilization might not have ascended to its then present heights. Where humans relied on disturbances of sound waves through the air that dissipated as quickly as they were emitted, the canines possessed an elegant method of communication based on olfaction. The scent particles, far more complex than any human could imagine, each contained a signature, like a fingerprint or a snowflake. Crude human communication crested with the creation of millions of words but relied on the reading of various intonations and meaning, which placed a large burden on the interpreter and also allowed for miscommunication. The scent particles, on the other hand, comprising a single scentima numbered in the thousands, each one a tiny signature that relayed the phrase, intonation, and context of the message. Distance was sometimes a challenge, but brief exclamations and phrases were robust enough to traverse miles. What was more, the scentimic particles, in part biological but generally inert and impervious to rapid degradation, gripped their surface for days and sometimes weeks. Obedient insects, part indifferent drones and part domesticated by the dogs, also aided in the dispersion of the scentimas. With the scentimas, the canines coordinated, planned, and organized into the body known as the Central Canine Government.

That day, the scentimas heralded the presence of the three other committee members: Sasha, a light-hearted but intelligent Siberian Husky; Chuckles, a Dachshund who hated his name, most of life, and all humans except his co-habitants; and Cooper, a Golden Retriever colored a rich, lustrous reddish brown with a penchant for the dramatic.

Properly briefed from the scentimas, Casey arrived and touched upon one related to a recurring problem. "The Yorkshire Terriers from the edge of town near the city are complaining once again that their interests are underrepresented." Casey snorted, and her disgust with this issue was apparent to the other dogs. "What, exactly, are they trying to achieve? What, specifically, is the problem?"

Chuckles interjected with a groan, followed by rigorous barks and some sniffling and snorting, "Does it matter? They'll never actually be happy. They need to accept their status as mini-canines and as close-mates of the humans instead of railing against their own inability to achieve greater things than they're capable of. The problem of the Wilds is still pressing."

"We always end up pushing their agenda to the side because of the Wilds," Casey said, cutting him off. "We will deal with the Wilds at another session. Today, we need to take care of our domestic agenda. It simply will not move the goals of the committee forward if we end up barking around the Wilds issue, which may never get solved, while we ignore the needs of our pack-friends."

Gently howling, Sasha offered, "I spoke with two very agitated Beagles yesterday, and they were saying that the Yorkies are disappearing."

"Disappearing," barked Cooper, "surely, they meant it in a figurative sense, as in disappearing from the mainstream canine agenda?"

"No," Sasha said. "The even stranger thing about the meeting was that the Beagles were insistent that the humans wanted the Yorkies gone, and that no signs for missing dogs have been spotted for the ones that disappeared. I checked, and the Canine Relocation Unit has not reported any Yorkshire Terriers requesting new humans or reporting lousy food, so they haven't shown up there, either. Yorkies almost never leave their human-mates."

Casey, paused for several moments as she absorbed the information, but stepped in before Cooper could extend one of his patented conspiracy theories. "Why don't we set up a meeting with the neighborhood representative to get the full story? It does us no good to throw theories out without any supporting evidence."

Casey tipped her nose into the air and sensed apprehension from Chuckles. Chuckles was not prone to being nervous and was unusually confident even when other committee members opposed him or when common sense rode against his ideas. In addition to their barking and direct communication, unspoken feelings and doubts would often manifest into additional scentimas through a snort or shudder that the dog would shed. The result was a complex series of whimpering, barking, and sniffing when each dog communicated.

Chuckles nervously ripped forward a few barks. "I did not think it relevant to our committee, but perhaps it does pertain to the Yorkie issue."

"Out with it Chuck," howled Sasha.

"Well, I was sniffing with a secretary ... ONLY a secretary, mind you, of one of the committee members of the Canine Health division. She was a very nonchalant German Shepherd and she maintained that there was an unusual spike in car deaths over the last six months for which the committee has no explanation. I was sure she was exaggerating, but she did mention it was in West-town near the city."

"That's the heart of Yorkie territory," added Cooper.

"Exactly."

"So, we have our explanation then," whimpered Sasha, "the Yorkies were hit by cars and, for whatever reason, the bodies have never been found. It's unusual, as our squirrel reports are fairly complete, but they're probably having some surveillance issues with all the recent bad weather. We had three thunderstorms just in the last week."

"It still doesn't explain the part about the human-mates wanting their Yorkies gone," Casey snuffled, "and now we've got more second-hand information that may not even be accurate. We need to meet with the West-town representative. He will likely have information on this issue."

"If you want, Casey," Sasha replied, "but it'll likely open up a den of troubles. The West-town representative will probably use the opportunity to push his platform and create a political maelstrom. We may get just as much misinformation as real information. He's up for re-election and is fighting a giant hairball of momentum from a well-liked Akita, who recently saved a puppy from a member of the Wilds."

"We just have to take that chance. There are too many unanswered questions. It is not very *carambee* of us to ignore the Yorkies when some might be missing under mysterious circumstances."[1]

"Odd if you ask me," added Cooper, "I'll have to chew on this matter a bit—"

"Then it's agreed," barked Chuckles. "We'll set it up for next week...let's move onto item two. Several of the Boxers are reporting favorable obedience training for some of the fresher pups in the town. I'd say this is an ideal opportunity to..."

Casey's attention trailed off until the meeting came to a close. She inhaled the air tentatively, attempting to glean more information from a West-town that was too far for scentimas to reach. Odd, indeed, she thought. Missing dogs, car deaths, human betrayal...odd, indeed...

[1] Carambee is a canine term that means a combination of loyalty and unity among all canines, i.e. a sense of brotherhood. Different contexts of these require the preservation of the original term.

WINGED WARNINGS

Casey's back yard was a combination exercise pen and meditation room. A chain-link fence ran parallel to and faced the house along the back, and a black aluminum fence ran along the remainder of the perimeter. A brick patio with a smattering of lawn furniture and a picnic table betrayed its purpose, and it was bordered with a small row of mulch and various plants amenable to a temperate climate. The rest was luscious green grass, just over an acre in totality.

Casey had a designated "area" within her human-mates' home. She could escape, however, to the serenity of the yard at any time because of a wonderfully insulated dog door, which kept the inside cozy from the cold and rain but allowed her access to the outside with a gentle push.

On this day, she ambled along her perimeter, gathering the various scentimas that comprised her mail. The breezes brought scentimas from the farthest reaches of her district and contained news, general information, and public service messages. The leaves and pollen spewed news from adjacent streets and neighborhoods, and symbiotic insects, like carrier pigeons to humans, mediated more official cables. Their canine masters easily directed them to various locales for the transmission of information and key reports. The grass itself was the mailbox. Newer scentimas, with fresh particles containing key phrases, alighted on the tips of the blades, while older messages sank closer to the ground and faded over time. When the canines snorted, it shuffled the scentimas and re-layered them as if marking them as "read" or "unread." With all of these tools at her disposal, Casey could easily keep track of the goings-on of her district and, sometimes, farther areas as well.

Several days loomed ahead of Casey prior to her meeting, but some pending background research still nagged her. She started with a clarification of the basic details of the West-town politician. She went to the southwest corner of the lawn, and two honeybees settled on the fence. A subtle blend of body movements and ear twitches mixed with snorts and a high-pitched whine relayed her directions to swing by a few canine-adopted houses near West-town to get the skinny on the representative.

As she sunned herself, she caught a breeze with a scentima forewarning the honeybees' return. The scentima was faintly hostile, and Casey realized that the West-town representative was not wellliked. Since breeze-borne scentimas are not sufficient for at-length elaboration on a subject, Casey knew she would have to bide her time until a pollinated bee returned.

She was halfway done checking for ticks when the honeybees returned with two brief summations:

Dear Senator Labrador-Casey,

Thank you for your interest in our district. I am a mixed Labrador/ German Shepherd/Akita male who works as liaison to several litter-watchers to help guide our young pups to endear themselves to our beloved human-mates. I did not vote for West-town Representative Spaniel-Lucky,[2] as I am a member of the Contrarian party, but I am familiar with his politics. Unfortunately, they hark back to the days before fences, when strict Submissivist policies were the norm. He hardly realizes the value of true friendship with our human-mates, and it is widely rumored that he associates with the nameless vermin. If true, it is hypocritical and not in the true spirit of carambee. It is also notoriously difficult to get an audience with him, despite the nature of his office. As I was telling the Bulldog Police last week when several of my scentima sticks were misplaced that...

---

2 It was customary to preface official letters to canine politicians with their title followed by their breed and hyphenated with the recipient's name. It was considered appropriate and customary to shorten the breed name to one word if necessary as canines are thought to be fond of brevity.

Casey skimmed the rest. Though it tended to ramble on and on about the obscure details of this mixed breed's life, it did tell her something about this Representative Lucky. If he was a strict Submissivist and was in danger of losing his seat to the Akita, he must be positively awful or corrupt, as West-town was known for being a Submissivist stronghold. Casey snorted at the thought of days long past when the Submissivists were in full control of all aspects of the canine government. They adhered to the notion that the key to prosperity was to blindly follow the human-mates and to entrust to them all aspects of canine existence. Submissivists were needed at one time because most properties were not secured, the Wilds were strong, and canine in-fighting left many wounded or dead.

As times changed, however, and more of the landscape turned from farmlands to suburbs, the Contrarian party grew out of a kinder notion of living alongside the human-mates. No longer was it considered necessary to tirelessly decipher every human move-ment and communication in the name of self-preservation. Though the world was more open, it was also safer. Casey was a Contrarian, and she believed strongly in endearment over blind faith in the human-mates. Her perfect Labrador features helped her attain this end, to be sure, but her attitude also helped shape this philosophy. Contrarians were happier canines, in her opinion. Still, though the Submissivists were a step backwards, it was shocking that Lucky, a Submissivist, could lose favor among those in his own party. The platform of the Submissivist party was changing, however, and Lucky perhaps found his supporters split as the Submissivists pushed their Canine First! agenda.

The nameless vermin were another matter. Rats, mice, gophers, and possums comprised this blanket term. Raccoons were also in the group until approximately three years ago when the Shared Garbage Amendment passed by a wide margin. Those species were never referred to individually for two reasons. First, because of the species gap, it was exceedingly difficult to translate their bizarre dialects, and few insects were capable of being go-betweens. Casey cocked her head in an attempt to think of the last canine that could translate more than a few random words of any of their languages. Second, they not only preyed on the humans, they generally disrupted the households. It was enough of a challenge to convince the human-mates that canines were necessary without any trouble from the outside. When the nameless vermin chewed wires, left droppings, and damaged drywall, it created a hostile environment for all non-human animals in the house. Also, they often did their dirty work at night, like a feline would, which left a rotten taste in any canine's mouth. No, the nameless vermin were not to be trusted or encour-aged. The mere mention of a canine politician with them was seen often enough in smear campaigns in heavily contested elections. Usually, it was in regard to a candidate not killing one when he had the chance or "harboring them" in the house without letting the authorities know. Never, to Casey's knowledge, has any canine, poli-tician or otherwise, been known to *associate* with them. It simply was not done.

Yet, here she had a dog who claimed it was "widely rumored" that a canine was doing just that. Surely the Akita challenger could easily take that seat now, but why would Lucky associate with these creatures? Their small size gave them access to areas that a dog might wish to explore, but the chipmunks, although temperamen-tal, often aided canines in that arena. Food was so plentiful that not one of the vermin could provide anything that a canine could reasonably tolerate. The only possible reason was subversion. The nameless vermin were known to be outstanding spies, and, when they were identified in a household, they were often gone at the onset of the investigation, leaving only their droppings and scraps of leftover, rancid food.

This information was volatile, and Casey laid down and sunned herself, sniffing the breeze, while she pondered this dreadful rumor. Some of the more ambitious members of the Contrarian party might want to run with this, displaying it to all canines as evidence of the lengths Submissivists would go to gain advantage. But the rumor could be false, in which case it was bait that Casey might not want to devour.

It would also need explanation. Staunch Submissivists would

howl, "And how would we even interact with these vermin, show me someone who could communicate with them beyond a phrase?" Then, the Contrarians, in turn, would be open to criticism that they themselves are associating with the vermin, for how else could they imagine that any canines would interact with the vermin? Then the Submissivists would say, "They are trying to paint us with the brush of their guilt! The Contrarians are associating with the vermin in attempts to open relations with them in other ways and trying to convince you, canine voters, 'See, we can learn from others, can interact with others, can share with others, not just the human-mates.'" Casey shook her head and the scenario disappeared from her mind. Throwing these sorts of accusations around was messy at best and disastrous at worst. The Contrarians were already brand-ed as "the amoral party," and the Submissivists retained a locked-jaw grip on morality issues. Most canine voters, of either party, would already pick the Contrarians as the party most likely to be sympathetic to the vermin, despite the fact Casey knew not one Contrarian who would even consider opening relations with them. Casey sighed, exasperated. She gnawed at another plan of action to tackle this rumor when a second scentima came in from the bees:

Dear Senator Labrador-Casey,
This is a most surprising and unwelcome intrusion into our neigh-borhood. For months, the Contrarians have ignored many of our issues, especially those pertaining to the Wilds. Now, you seek information about our representative, who works tirelessly on our behalf. I will answer your inquiry, however, in the spirit of carambee.
Representative Spaniel-Lucky has thankfully pushed his Canine First! plan, knowing that it will make us safer and hap-pier. As you probably know, we continue to push for puppy over-sight only from a distance, instead of the meddling fashion in which you now indoctrinate our young. Rep. Lucky showed us that the Yorkies' disappearances are the fault of our flawed sys-tem and that such occurrences never happened years ago, even when we had fewer barriers and more intrusions from the Wilds.

Hopefully, you will ratify the Canine First! plan should it reach the Senate, and I trust...

Casey snorted in disgust. She had hoped to receive some objective information from her two probes, but instead she received rhetoric spanning the two parties. She would have to look more into the Canine First! plan, as it would probably be on her next committee agenda, assuming it passed the House. Likely, the Canine First! plan was another name for an array of directives that the Submissivists have been pushing to separate canines from humans, part of the "re-branding" of their party. Only a snout-to-snout meeting would suffice with Representative Lucky, but she still felt unprepared. Casey knew that if she was unprepared, she could do serious damage to her office and her own agenda. She wished she had more time with which to obtain more background information, but she also wanted to clear this issue from her agenda.

Casey got up from her sunny corner of the yard. More scentimas came in with various reports, but she was too distracted with these new concerns. Tomorrow they would make an impromptu visit. She snuffled a scentima sent out to Cooper to meet with her tomorrow. She stretched out pensively.

She whirled her yellowish-golden body around to re-enter the home when she saw a black bird perched like stone at the far end of her yard. Not like a predator and more like a protector, she bounded over, set to unleash the low growl in the back of her throat. The bird was looking upwards at the sky when she initially spotted it, but it turned its black, stoic eyes towards her as she approached. The breeze seemed almost to deaden around her as she drew near it.

Casey did not recognize the bird, but it appeared to be... yes, she believed it was a crow. She knew from old puppy stories that crows were ornery and not to be taken lightly. Before her neighborhood was a suburb, she was told, miles of farm were haven to these winged beasts. Though they did not live in communion with the canines, they were not parasitic. "Leaving the skies to things of the sky" was one of the lines from the charter that set the boundaries of the Central Canine Government, but this crow was on *her* fence, and so it was squarely in her yard and in her district. Casey had every right to confront this animal.

When she was nearly upon it, the crow arched its head and snapped its wings outward and then back towards its body. This action startled Casey, and she unleashed a warning growl, giving what she knew was an inter-species challenge.

"SQWAUKKK!!!" the bird fired back, "WESTTTTTTTTTTOOOWW-WWN!!!"

Had she heard the crow correctly? Casey knew it was rare to decipher the birds' language, but barked back what she believed would be a reply, "What about West-town? What do you want here, crow? You have the trees and the sky and there surely is no farm land here for you now." Maybe the crow was old and senile or was lost, Casey mused.

The crow stared into Casey's own with its dark, vacuous eyes. It snapped its wings out and in again, without giving any indication that it had understood a single word Casey had said. "SQWWW-WAAAAAUUK!! WESSSTTT-TTOOOWWWN WILL BE GOOO—SQWWW-WAAAUKKK, SQWAAAUUKK, BE GOOOOOOOONE! SQWWWWAUUKK!"

Casey growled and the hair along her spine bristled. "What do you mean, crow! West-town is not gone! I am a ranking senator, and I demand an answer." The crow did not respond. Casey barked a command to some bees resting on a rosebush. "You there, find out what this crow means!" The bees mobilized towards Casey to pick up a scentima from the crow as Casey turned to confront it.

The crow remained staring that dead, vacant stare for just a few more seconds. Then, noiselessly, it dipped its head down just slightly and took off.

Casey bounded through her dog door and barked unrelentingly. Finally, her human-mates acquiesced. They snapped on her leash to bring her to the dog park.

DOG PARK

Sasha was already at the enclave that was Casey's beloved dog park. The dog park was a heavily wooded three acre lot where Casey was off leash, and she could commune easily with various government agencies. Even on the hottest days, Casey could be assured of comfort and shade. After being let off leash, she perused the area and briefed Sasha about the events in the back yard. Sasha scratched her ear with a back paw.

"I just don't see how a crow could have something to do with the missing Yorkies," concluded Sasha. "Maybe it was senile?"

"I cannot help but think they are in some way related, Sasha. I racked my brain trying to think of some connection between the Yorkies and West-town. I just can't shake the feeling that the crow's appearance must mean something. First the Yorkies, and now all of West-town?"

"Maybe the crow meant that the Yorkies are gone and confused the translation, and so just confirmed what we already know."

"The crow was very clearly talking about West-town," Casey barked sharply in reply. "It even repeated the phrase West-town, and I can't imagine the words for West-town and Yorkies being similar in any species dialect."

A canine page pleasantly interrupted their conversation. A canine page was usually a dog of a small breed meant to serve as informant across different committees and between different legislative branches. The noticeably high-strung Toy Poodle came bounding towards them, practically hopping in step while delivering his message. "Senators Labrador-Casey and Husky-Sasha, pardon my interruption. The Minority Barker of the Senate, Senator Beagle-Juniper, requests the pleasure of your presence and counsel regarding a matter of the Senate Committee of Canine Defense."

Casey's floppy ears stood up and bolted far forward, then reflexively relaxed as she mentally composed her reply. "I am sure Senator Juniper is looking for Representative Labrador-Brassy. He is on the sister committee in the House, that of Canine Discovery, Surveillance, and Defense." Casey made a quick snuffle, "Although we are both Labradors, my little Poodle page, he is a black Labrador and is male. You do know the difference, do you not?" Sasha shook her head to hide her amusement.

Sasha barked, adding, "My page, we are on the Committee of Inter-Canine Communication, and, as you are no doubt aware, we hardly deal with military strategy. Even with the Wilds, we always seek a diplomatic solution, if only so that your honorable senator has less in his bowl."

The Toy Poodle, with greyish white fine curly hair that almost looked both dirty because of the grey tinge and silky because of the shine off of it, seemed to be jittery and nervous. No doubt the running back and forth among committees damaged the coat over time. Blinking rapidly and batting his front paws on the dirt, the page forced out a reply between nervous yips, "B-b-but Senators, Sen-sen-senator Beagle-Juniper was quite clear. H-h-he said, 'Fetch me the t-t-two head senators on the Committee of Inter-Canine Communication,' I-I-I looked you up myself, Senators, I am sure he means you two, if it please you Senators Casey and Sasha."

Casey and Sasha exchanged sideways looks. Sasha's ears bent backwards, and her mouth betrayed a glint of teeth, reflecting her disdain for the powerful Senator Juniper. When Sasha had won her Senate seat six months ago, she ran on a platform that was against war with the Wilds. Many of her constituents served as reserves in the canine military, and during the First Canine War thirty years ago, heavy losses plagued her district. The near annihilation of that district nearly split the Central Canine Government into two parts, requiring years of cultivation to form stronger bonds with the humans in order to replenish their numbers. It was thought that this brief time of discontinuity cultivated the strength of the Wilds. Despite their key role in the military, they were notoriously opposed to conflict, sweeping Sasha into office. Juniper slinked into her yard one evening shortly after victory to give her a key role in a bipartisan bill that primarily gave dogs of her district prefer-ence with health services. What Juniper failed to disclose was a short addendum that would be added minutes before the vote that extended the duration of military service for all canines that affected her district most. The canine press buried Sasha, and there was nearly a recall. It was an important lesson that Sasha never forgot: beware Beagles bearing gifts.

Following nearly a minute of silence, the breeze picked up, ruffling Sasha and Casey's fur. "Well, we had better go see what he wants," Sasha snapped. "It's probably nothing of major importance."

Casey snorted affirmation. Too many surprises over the past two days, she thought to herself. She, as most politicians did, loathed surprises because of the possibility that she would be exposed to controversial situations that forced her to shoulder unpleasant responsibilities, often on the periphery of her knowledge and expertise. And Juniper, despite his size, was a political bully. Though formally a member of the Submissivists, his politics bridged both Submissivist and Contrarian principles. The Senate had a decisive Contrarian majority, but the Submissivists dominated the defense committees in the Senate and the House. The Submissivists picked Juniper unanimously because he was bipartisan, bold, and had seniority. Juniper was aging fast, Casey thought; if memory served, he was nearly eleven years old.

All these thoughts clicked along as she trotted behind Sasha up a moderately steep path to a corner of the dog park reserved for debates and decisions by dominance.[3] This also made Juniper unusual. Most canines on the committees of defense where military decisions were made were larger breeds. Juniper was especially adept at Dominance matches, despite his size, although he was a fairly beefy Beagle.

As Casey and Sasha approached, Juniper stood with ears at attention. He almost looked angry, Casey thought. No doubt it was his intimidating impression that helped set his reputation.

---

3 Decisions by dominance, where two dogs fought with a pact not to puncture skin, were often used for draws within committees regarding bill passages and controversial legislation.

Juniper, with typical tan and white Beagle coloring, was almost twenty-five pounds of Beagle. In contrast to Casey, he did not appear overweight. Casey came out from behind Sasha and stood just in front of her, but off-center, indicating the hierarchy in the committee. Juniper cocked his head in greeting.

"Senators Casey and Sasha," Juniper brusquely barked. "I am so glad you could come so soon. I trust Thimbles briefed you a bit on the situation and that you can see why I requested a snout-to-snout?"

Thimbles, the page, cowered behind a nearby tree. Clearly, Casey had scared him a bit when she had accused him of contacting the wrong canines. Thimbles had obviously done only part of his job, and he shook as if he had just emerged from an ice cold lake.

"Actually, Senator Juniper, we confused Thimbles a bit I think, and we were not exactly briefed."

Juniper took two wide-stance steps towards Thimbles and thrust his neck forward. Thimbles attempted to shrink into the ground. Casey half expected him to try to dig a hole in which to hide. Juniper cocked his head back at Casey and Sasha, "I am deeply sorry for my page's incompetence, my honorable colleagues. The matter is an unusual one, and I told Thimbles to brief you so as not to totally swat you on the snout with this, so to speak." In public, Juniper was often overly formal. Many canines snuffled that the formality melted away behind closed dog doors.

Casey knew that Juniper was bipartisan but was also self-sufficient. He earned respect across both parties because he was remarkably resourceful for a small dog, and even Casey herself had admitted that Juniper had a sound military mind. If he was looking for her and Sasha's counsel, he likely either needed it or he was trying to send a political message about the matter. "What is it Juniper?" Part of Casey's appeal from the broader support for the Contrarians lay in her departure from the stiffness of the older politicians.

Juniper shifted a bit, and his hair stood up above his eyes, "We have been tracking the Wilds' movements for almost two months. We feel they are readying themselves for a major offensive. The magnitude of this offensive is not completely known but may dwarf that of the Trans-Canine Wars thirty years ago.[4] I will not lie to you, Senators, we have major gaps in our surveillance, which I have discussed with Representative Brassy at length on three separate occasions in the last two weeks alone. Finally, after I barked myself hoarse at the last joint meeting, he suggested we needed to go a different direction. We need to consult those of the air, the birds, in particular the birds known as the—"

"Crows!?" barked Sasha. Her bushy fur seemed to double in size. She, at once, scolded herself. Sasha loathed the notion of aiding Juniper even if it was a simple matter of facilitating conversation.

"Crows...?" Juniper looked confused as he flexed his ears. "No, no...why would you think that? No, no...Robins. We need help opening up a line of communication with the robins. Why would you think crows would even be helpful? Have you even seen one? I saw one eight years ago and I was just waking up from a nap under my favorite tree in the back yard. I still think it might've been a dream."

Casey sighed and she peeked at Sasha, whose nose was bent a little low. Sometimes she wondered how Sasha was such an adept politician when she had such difficulties keeping issues close to her snout. She had not explicitly told Sasha not to mention the crow, but Casey did not achieve prominence by being careless. "I thought I saw a crow earlier," barked Casey. "I thought it rather odd. I think the crow was senile or lost."

Juniper sniffed at Casey, no doubt trying to pick up scentimas that might divulge further clues to the story. Casey felt it rude, but she knew that Juniper liked to throw his weight around. "Odd," said Juniper, glancing behind him at a conclave filled with several other dogs. He likely had other issues to address. "Do you think you can find a canine that can speak to the robins? We need a new tack."

---

4 Most canine scholars used the First Canine War and Trans-Canine War interchangeably, but it was felt that the term, 'Trans-Canine' implied that the enemy, the Wilds, were some sort of subspecies of canines.

Talk about the edge of her expertise! It was not an unreasonable request, as there were no committees or governmental organizations dedicated to translation across other animal species, but this was an unorthodox use of her talents. Even though Casey had multiple contacts, the skies were the dominion of the birds. She would not know where to start. On the other hand, success here could elevate her status as well as shed some light on this crow issue.

Casey brought her snout to Juniper's and dipped her head a bit in both deference and acceptance, "I will see what I can ferret out, Juniper. I cannot promise even a small success. You know as well as I that this is a foray into unsniffed territory."

Juniper widened his stance a bit; now he almost appeared comically bold. "Thank you, Senators. I look forward to anything you can find. Please excuse me." Juniper brought his snout forward and dipped a bit farther in honor of Casey and Sasha. In turn, Casey and Sasha returned the gesture. Casey knew he initiated the formality so as to receive the pleasure of deference from them. Juniper's ego was, after all, unmatched. He then turned abruptly and walked away, his tail held high. They heard him talking to what was likely his support staff. "Canines, in the spirit of carambee, we need to know three things…"

Juniper's growls and barks faded as Sasha and Casey retreated to get some water.

"This West-town representative," Casey finally growled, "I have a feeling he may know a bit about inter-species communication."

Sasha tipped her head into the air and let out a faint howl, "Uggghhh, with the nameless vermin, I can't even imagine."

The breeze felt inviting to her coat. "Sadly," Casey tilted her head back at Sasha, "I think we may be exposed to more than a few unimaginable situations in the next few days."

WEST-TOWN

The Central Canine Government had over seventy districts, each with one senator and a variable number of representatives. To the south and east of their territory, four and five lane highways made up the borders. Casey's home and district lay in the southeastern portion of the territory, close to the eastern border. Quite appropriately, there was South-town, East-town, West-town, and North-town. These names delineated general areas that encompassed many districts. Sasha's district was fairly central and shaded to the north a bit too. Her district and Casey's sandwiched the dog park. West-town was a far trek.

The dew was still on the morning grass. After a brief but satisfying breakfast, Casey padded out through the dog door, waited the requisite half hour for her human-mates to leave, and then slipped through a hole obscured in the far back corner of the yard. A hole near a wood pile that was dug during her campaign served as a means for escape for urgent matters. The fog on Casey's home street was thick this morning, and Cooper emerged from it to greet Casey. Cooper was acting as bodyguard, though his breeding was far from such inclinations.

"I don't know, Casey," Cooper whimpered, his golden coat seeming to almost shimmer with nervousness to reflect his mood, "maybe we should involve the B.P.[5] If the nameless vermin are heavily involved with the West-town representative, who knows what types of other alliances he has formed?"

Casey yipped sharply, curling her lip, "Relax, Cooper, what type of alliances would there be to fear?"

Almost whimpering silently and stepping slowly to indicate fear, "Well, there is the matter of the Wilds…Sasha told me about the big offensive."

"*That*," Casey said, "is not yet confirmed. Juniper and his pups are constantly drumming up the next major offensive. As part of

5 Bulldog Police – the main enforcement body of the Central Canine Government

the Committee for Defense, they need all sorts of reasons to garner the most pup-power,[6] and the fear entrenched deep in our fur is a fear of the Wilds. They are really just banking on our most base characteristics."

After walking nearly all day, they came upon a more sparsely populated area of their territory. As opposed to Casey's neighborhood, where the houses were often two stories and brick or sided, this particular area had mostly one story houses, mainly of wood, set back farther and often with the houses half-obscured by an alcove of trees. The change in the neighborhoods was gradual, but it seemed glaringly obvious now, as if someone had suddenly changed the background reel.

"Have you thought about how we would open communications with the robins?" inquired Cooper.

Casey snuffled. She paused first to tilt her head into the air to pick up any scentimas that might indicate misdirection. This was, after all, only her third trip to West-town, and only her second on official government business. The first had been during campaigning for a Contrarian challenger to another Submissivist's seat. She barked, "I thought it was silly at first, but the more I rattle the idea around in my bowl, the more I feel it is our only option."

Cooper started to pant along with Casey as the sun started to set. "I don't like the way this smells, Casey, but tell me."

"The other," Casey's barks dropped to a whimper, "wanyamas."[7]

"Ahhh," Cooper became more chipper with his barks, "the felines. Why would you hesitate?" Cooper lived with one feline and often forgot that such associations were uncommon.

---

6   The "monetary" system of canines was the designation of puppies under various jurisidictions. By gaining more puppies, the amount of attention, food, treats, and status granted by the humans was proportionately more. Thus, the amount of puppies was the proxy for real wealth in the canine system at that time.

7   Wanyama loosely translates as domesticated animals, and specifically usually refers to cats, the other common domesticated animal of the time. Canines had no word for domesticated animals because their history only dated back to the time of domestication, and canines had no reference point to realize their prior undomesticated time.

"We've got several working theories about Yorkies disappearing and no real credible stories or witnesses to explain the incidents. The feline political agenda is our polar opposite, and yet, they've arrived to a similar degree of endearment with the humans. Yet the felines do not share our sense of carambee. There is no telling where their true devotions lie or how far they will diverge from us politically in the long run." Casey gave a long, thoughtful lick around her mouth in between pants as she glanced sidelong at Cooper. He seemed to be satisfied with the explanation.

"So, asking Mittens is out of the question? Would you rather go for an Alley?"

"Actually," continued Casey, "I've been battling that myself. We have bits and pieces of stories, but we're not entirely sure of all the actors. Making unorthodox political moves like going to rogue felines may attract more attention than not. It is probably best if we approach Mittens first."

Cooper, between pants, begrudgingly, "Fine. You know she is a civilian, though?" He had little affection for the cat.

"Felines are so mercenary in mentality that it matters little, anyway. To survive and thrive in their community, one would have to be an individual foremost. Government, to the wanyamas, is unnecessary and an intrusion, but to stay current, they need to have a paw on the pulse of the community. I am sure that government is hardly discussed in the household, right?" Casey cast a sidelong glance at Cooper. Cooper snorted and shook his head pensively.

"Little is said."

"Good," Casey acknowledged both to herself and to her companion. She was always concerned about the risk of breach of security in the house, but Cooper was unbelievably transparent, even for a canine, and she was generally confident that he never took his work into the human-mate home.

"Outside," Casey said as she twitched her ears to his direction to be certain that she had his full attention, "outside only, bring up the matter of translation. Do not inform Mittens of the true intent. If she thinks we are behind the treat in this matter, she may use what little political connection she has to maximize the feline advantage. The last thing we need is to turn a diplomatic problem into a full-on inter-species conflict."

"I could relate it to the missing Yorkies. Talk about how we are exploring another avenue for investigation."

"No. Mittens is not bright, but she's not stupid. I'm not even entirely sure myself why we haven't turned this Yorkies issue over to the Bulldogs to open up an official investigation. I guess I'm still holding out hope that this matter turns out to be minor, although the more heavily we get involved, the more we are playing into Human Doctrine.[8] Until we parcel this into whatever risk category it falls into, I wouldn't mention it. Tell Mittens that we are broadening our diplomatic relations in response to the fact that the Wilds are doing the same. If she pries, then—"

"Make something up?" Cooper barked questioningly.

Casey whimpered humorously. Cooper was most definitely transparent, but he was also adept at making himself seem transparent while hiding key information, an incredibly unique and valuable skill for any politician. Mittens likely thought he was no more significant in the world of government than the hairballs she coughed up. It would no doubt benefit Cooper to cultivate this attitude in Mittens.

As the two canines trotted along, the trees became more sparse. The homes had various architecture but were uniformly small and had poorly kept yards. A few flies flitted past Casey, carrying scentimas that acknowledged that Casey was only a street away from Lucky's post. Casey tucked one leg underneath herself as she sat and whirled on Cooper.

"Okay," Casey barked softly, with her ears at attention to pick up on anyone that might be listening. "Keep your nose, ears, and eyes open for any unusual behavior. I'm not sure what we are going to find around here or, for that matter, whether there is even 'anything to find.'"

---

8   The Human Doctrine was discovered by canines hundreds of years ago as testament to overly aggressive human intervention, the essential gist of the doctrine states, "When you make a big deal out of something, it becomes a big deal." The avoidance of this policy was rapidly coming out of favor at the time of these matters.

A few dozen feet away, a side street opened up. It was a short cul-de-sac, and had six homes, all fairly set back. At the corner of this street, on opposite sides of the street entrance, stood a thin Rottweiler mix and an orange cat. Their general appearance seemed to match that of the shoddy homes on the street.

Casey and Cooper kept their eyes on these two animals as they neared. The feline, the wanyama, noticed the canines first and turned, in its sitting position, to face them. Its dark orange tail swished pensively from side to side. The Rottweiler mix barked a curt but civil greeting to the approaching dignitaries.

"We are here to see Representative Lucky," barked Casey. "I am Senator Labrador-Casey, head of the Committee of Inter-Canine Communication. This is Senator Cooper, also a sitting member on that committee. We have business with the representative regarding matters both public and private." Casey adjusted her front paws in an unspoken acknowledgment that it should have not been necessary to divulge any information regarding the nature of her business, and that what was said was said out of courtesy.

Surprisingly, the feline responded first, "About time we had some semblance of a central response. The Yorkie disappearances are not solving themselves, but Representative Lucky has matters well in hand. I doubt he needs your counsel."

Cooper bristled a bit, his eyebrows rising in shock at the feline's impertinence. In a direct show of force and cross-species' dominance, he padded forward until he lorded over the cat. His response was calm, however, as he allowed his nonverbal communication to direct the tone, "Cat, once the matter comes up in committee and has been submitted, we will investigate it however we choose, and, indeed, whether to investigate the matter at all. I trust your informality reflects the mere distance from the higher chain of command of which, I hope, you are nearer the bottom. It would be a shame if we had to investigate Lucky for corruption matters."

Cooper's demeanor did not phase the feline. She yawned and, without looking at the Rottweiler mix, mewed, "Stucco, go inform Representative Lucky that he has *central* dignitaries here. You know," she said, redirecting her piercing feline gaze at the massive Retriever, "it is a pity that size is clearly still the dominating force among your species."

Casey, still convinced that the whole meeting was off on the wrong paw because of their pre-briefing she had mentioned earlier, knew that the feline was hinting at something that was obviously different about West-town. She also quickly surmised that said difference likely explained the feline's involvement.

"I hope you realize kitten," Casey clearly resorting to terms that were outright insulting, "that since the Non-Confrontation Treaty of 2021, dog-on-cat violence has actually only risen as the language of the law only serves to dissuade affected parties from reporting said violence. In addition, there is little desire by our Bulldog Force to even investigate matters in fear of rupturing the treaty." Something about the senator Labrador's frame seemed more imposing on the cat as her short hair did not easily hide the bulk of Casey's frame. The orange, bold feline did back off a foot...maybe two.

After a moment, Stucco returned. "E-e-esteemed Senators, Representative Lucky is honored and pleased to receive you. I will escort you to his yard." Stucco seemed unsure of the initial address, as if he had been hastily coached in formalities before returning. Ah, things were so different far from the central hub of the government, where even the gophers and chipmunks had honorable tendencies!

"Show us the way, canine-friend," Casey barked.

Stucco padded towards the house at the end of the cul-de-sac. The fence to the side of the house was weather-worn and a dark, unnatural brown; the wood was nearly rotted. Stucco came up near a thorny plant and pulled at it gently to reveal a large hole. He sat, giving the honor of entrance to the two senators.

Casey trotted forward, but Cooper stopped her. "Senator Casey, allow me to enter first...ummm just in case." Cooper did not state his reservations outright, but the aim was clear.

A brief hemming and hawing ensued for Casey but she acquiesced, "Go ahead, Cooper," she yipped. She sat on her haunches on the opposite side of the hole of Stucco, who appeared frightened. What was he concerned about? Casey made a mental note to inquire of Lucky how he could make such inept decisions for his personal staffing.

Casey watched the very furry tail of the Golden disappear and crawled under herself. Lucky's back yard was dingy. It was small, too, barely fifteen to twenty feet at its widest. The yard was a small semi-circle, backed completely by forest. Casey saw that a chain-link fence was set fifty yards deep into the woods, but that the forest expanded to no apparent end. Old, muddy, used-up young human-mate toys were strewn at one far end of the yard, and Lucky sat with his head up and ears and eyes at attention. He was an orangish-tan and brown with large areas of white, a Spaniel per-haps two-thirds Casey's size.

The house stood three stories high, hulking over the puny yard. It felt nearly twice as tall as it was wide. The paint was chipping all over, from the wood under the windows to the greyish colored back porch. It seemed almost to creak in the gentle wind. The lat-tice under the porch was coming off from the supporting structure. Beyond the lattice was darkness. A typical older home from West-town, Casey thought to herself.

"Senator Labrador-Casey, I am very happy to have you here. I wish I had known you were coming, I could have had a canine escort for you at the halfway mark. The human-mates' roadways can be confusing," Lucky barked.

"Are you sure, Representative Lucky, that you would not have chosen a feline escort for us?" Casey growled curtly back.

Lucky yipped a laugh, "Ha! Shiva is a piece of work, no? This may sound surprising to you, but it helps to appear so desperate for staffing, that I have to resort to felines for aid. She is a most excel-lent deterrent, for unconventional reasons, of course."

"Although not explicitly forbidden, staffing felines is not in alignment with general custom, Representative," Cooper chimed in, chiding Lucky as one chides a misbehaving puppy.

Lucky stood up and faced Cooper, "You centralists do not real-ize the gravity of our situation," he barked. "We are so close to the Wilds, the *real* Wilds, that we must constantly appraise our situa-tion. We would need an army of Dobermans, Rottweilers, and Pit bulls to even contemplate turning the Wilds away, so I staff felines and allow my district to appear so weak as to be completely unappetizing."

"Not so unappetizing that dogs can't still go missing," Casey barked back, "Maybe you know something about Yorkies that did the same? And the Wilds are nothing but undocumented and lawless strays. If it's them you are worried about—" Casey could see she was starting to strike a nerve with Lucky and regrouped, "But...we are here to address your problem. The Yorkies have become a top concern, and Senator Cooper and I are seeing first-paw how we can be of assistance before we turn the matter over to Bulldog authorities." Casey barked further, "As for your insistence regarding the Wilds, who are always real to us, we are well aware of your proximity to the outskirts of the city and the expanse of uncharted lands, but we need to focus on the Yorkies for now—"

"Ohh, Casey," Lucky yipped, jumping up as if a switch had flipped within him, "you dolt of a Senator, *those* Wilds are nothing to us. I am speaking of the *real* Wilds. The *fananas* terrorize us from the woods, so much so that even the human-mates fear them. Do you hear young human-mates laughing out in the streets? These toys are relics. Only older human-mates and farmers with guns stay in my district. And the Yorkies you refer to in all likelihood left willingly, no doubt out of a sense of self-preservation. I answer now to those who continue to live in fear of the fananas."

The hair along Casey's spine instinctively stood on end. "The fananas are a legend. Not one pup or canine has seen a fanana in decades. Our human-mates drove them away and made a pact with our species of friendship and protection. The fananas would have to have such numbers to threaten even one neighborhood, never mind all of canine-dom. Even if they did have the numbers, the Wilds of the city would have rounded them up and run them down out of necessity."

"How little you know," Lucky growled back. "If you don't believe me, stay the night and see for yourself. A fanana comes nearly every night to watch me. I have become the last feeble link in a chain to keep them away, and that fence has not kept them from entering the neighborhood. They take whatever they can round up, and all the animals in the district come to this yard at night so that we can watch over and protect one another. I have felines on my staff so that if fananas breached security during the day, that the response could be more quickly mobilized."

The two senators sat back on their haunches, absorbing what they heard. Many stories circulated about the age of the fananas. Passed verbally through hundreds of generations of canines, it was difficult to parse out what was real and what was fantastical legend. Some stories claimed that the fananas were merely a subspecies of canine that rebelled against greater canine-dom. Others claimed that they miscalculated the bond between human and canine, paying the ultimate price as a result. Parent dogs scared their puppies from wandering at night by telling them the fananas had special abilities to smell wandering puppies. Other bizarre stories claimed that the fananas were the common descendant of the felines and canines, and that they had the most shameful and lethal characteristics of both: the cunning and stealth of a cat with well developed canine pack instincts. Some religious figures in the canine lay population claimed that fananas were the dead souls of dogs that defied humans, and that they stalked the land to wreak revenge. All the stories shared a common element: fear. Casey flicked her gaze in Cooper's direction. Behind him, an innocent bird startled.

Cooper's fur instinctively raised in anticipation. The big Golden senator brusquely bumped Lucky as he passed him to take in the scents of the near grounds. Turning frequently to glance at Lucky and dipping his snout to the ground, Cooper barked from the chain-link fence. "There is nothing here. A few older scentimas from canines, likely constituents of the representative here. There's also some bird, and lots of feline," he drank in the fence post again with his nose, "yes, *lots* of feline." Confidence reigned in his tone, but Casey could read subtler body language that conveyed some doubt.

Lucky let out yips of laughter that bore a manic tinge. He was afraid, Casey thought. "I assure you, Senators, the fananas have left their scentimas, but they are faint and subtle, in tune with the natural surroundings. You think you pick up a slightly heavy maple scent or goldenrod, and both might be fanana. Their scentimas disappear rapidly, and I have the felines patrol the borders at night and in the morning, marking the territory in hopes of establishing our territorial limits. Those scents *are* there, but how can you possibly recognize that which you have never sniffed?"

Casey had not considered that conundrum. She shook her head, barking, "Where are your human-mates? How do they not bring you in for the night? You make it sound as if these homes are abandoned, but I see the remnants of human-mate occupation. They are still here, and you cannot convince me that they are oblivious to the encroachment on their domain. They erect barriers to keep from one another, surely a fanana would spark an outpouring of activity?"

"My human-mates left me, Senator, and I have marked this territory as my own. I rely on the hospitality of human-mates around the neighborhood for food and water. The human-mates are no longer paying attention, not in West-town. Canines run amok year-round here, and only the daily food bowl marks a canine as the companion of a human-mate. The human-mates are blind to our plight and they are occupied, constantly occupied with non-canine concerns and attachments."

"Lies," growled Casey, "I refuse to believe it. Tending to us is one of the prime reasons why we chose to co-exist with th—"

"We chose? *We* chose?" Lucky growled back in disbelief. "You Contrarians have poisoned canines across the land with such nonsense. We no more chose the humans than we can control the birds of the sky or the fish in the streams. It is understanding our true role that has led me to push the Canine First! legislation, calling for our ultimate freedom, rather than shackling us to the whims of the humans." Lucky finished the last phrase with a curling of his upper lip defining his aggression and contempt for the human-mates.

Lowering her snout and, for the first time in the encounter, taking a stance exhibiting her superior status, Casey pawed at the air in front of Representative Lucky, "Part of the oath of office, Representative Lucky," Casey growled, "was honoring the commitment to advance the canine agenda for the good of all dogs, irrespective of your personal vendettas. I will stay to see your so-called fanana, but I will no longer listen to this treasonous talk."

Slowly sitting on his haunches, Lucky sniffed the air, and a small gnat buzzed almost noiselessly past his nose. He cocked his head, listening. The sun sat low in the sky and cast low-angle beams through the thick woods in the back of the forest, eerily illuminating the lattice underneath the porch of the house. Cooper whined a bit in nervous anticipation, and as the gnat flew away, Lucky slicked around his snout with a slow snap as his tongue pulled back into his mouth, "You do not have to listen to me any longer, esteemed Senator Casey. The gnat has told me a fanana is coming."

"Then we will wait," Casey said.

The minutes dragged as Casey padded near Cooper, who stood, panting, near the chain-link fence. She turned to appraise the distance from the wooden fence entrance and surmised, should escape be necessary, the distance was not small but manageable. Casey and Cooper stood like marble statues peering into the oncoming darkness. The woods, like a symphony playing on a broken radio, would occasionally explode with brief chattering of birds and insects only to die down a few minutes later.

The minutes dragged on. No fananas. Casey snuffled and turned her broad Labrador head to watch Lucky, who stood behind her. He sat noiselessly, intent on the land beyond the fence. She just at that time noticed that there was a Noah's Ark of animals in the yard, all kinds: chipmunks, multiple cats and other dogs, although mostly from smaller breeds, and even a few squirrels. They all were huddled in small cliques, near the latticework of the porch, trying to blend into its mesmerizing background. She turned to Cooper, who twitched his ears forward. There was fear in this neighborhood.

The scentima came over Casey, and it enveloped her nose, giving off a familiar, but slightly noxious odor. It smelled *canine*, and Casey became hopeful that a large stray dog was going to come out of those woods. Cooper then picked it up a brief millisecond after Casey and softly whimpered and shifted position protectively a bit closer to Casey. Casey shot him a stern look that said, "Keep quiet."

Then the grey beast appeared. It was huge and long and lean. A large triangular head and pointy snout slung low near the ground as it approached. It or he or she was quiet. The ears were erect, and its eyes looked knowledgeable and unforgiving. The beast seemed to possess the ferocity of the meanest feline, but shared its shape with that of a canine. Its coat was varying shades of grey and white, and its long, bushy tail stuck straight out parallel to its spine. The beast skulked to the fence, disturbing little ground. As it came within ten or twenty feet or so, it caught the eyes of Casey and Cooper, both of which were wide with disbelief. Fear welled in the pit of Casey's stomach: they were real.

"Senator Casey," Lucky whimpered, "we never stay so close. I do not know their customs, and I fear you are antagonizing it into a conflict that we cannot win. My feline scouts told me that three and possibly four more of them are waiting barely a hundred yards deeper into the forest. It is typical. They *never* travel alone, and they dare opposition wherever they go. Please retreat with me. Please, I beg of you, Senator." Lucky's pleas hissed into Casey's ears.

Casey's tongue was stone and would not move. She had locked onto the eyes of the fanana, and though it was a beast rivaling the Great Danes and Irish Wolfhounds in size, she knew it was still canine and was determined to know its purpose. Why did it stare so? Casey's mind raced to come up with a plan of action that wouldn't enrage the beast. Cooper stepped back, pulling Casey into the moment. "Cooper, stand your ground," she barked softly, "this animal does not need to think we fear it."

"You should fear me, puppy," the fanana responded, in Casey's language. The grey behemoth strode up to the fence. My gosh, Casey thought to herself, it was so effortless in its movements. It had a thick accent, almost as if it slurred its words, especially when the word "puppy" oozed from its mouth. "We are the true canines of this planet. Not some bastardized, weakened version that is suppliant to those pathetic and selfish humans. Humans have driven us from the nearby hills in the efforts to further parasitize this land, and now we seek new territory. I am amazed how many of you pseudo canines there are, and how pathetically diverse your lot is. It is as if half of you never stop being puppies." The fanana drew out her last word, which devolved into laughter.

"I am Senator Labrador-Casey and I represent the Central Canine Government with all its authorities and powers both implied and explicit in that position," Casey barked, putting up a brave front. She knew it to be true; she did carry a considerable weight of power behind her, just not at this moment, and not with a soft-hearted Golden serving as her bodyguard. "Do you hear me? So be warned: whatever you think of us, you owe us the allegiance fitting your canine heritage."

"I AM THE CANINE HERITAGE!" exploded the fanana. "We are the beginning, and we will be the end because we are survivors and have learned what not one of you domesticated fools have figured out: self-sufficiency. We were here before all of you, and we will be here when the humans finally tire of you and abandon you!"

Casey's fur was fluffed out to its max along her spine, "Alright, *beast*," she growled, "what do you want? What is your aim? I have no care for your wild theories and your pretentions of authority over us. I know our current structure and have lived and thrived in it, and we are at the helm of conquering even the strays and the law-less among us, so you and your... pals," she harrumphed towards the woods behind her, "can either state your business clearly or I will take the steps necessary to ensure that we make the business agenda for you." Casey gulped, hoping that the bluff would work.

"We want," the fanana whispered silently and it crept with its snout almost touching the fence, "to feeeeed." With that last word, the animal leapt over the fence and landed neatly behind Casey.

Casey had whirled in anticipation of the leap and landed a deep bite on its upper right leg, near the shoulder. The fanana growled and Casey twisted the wound before letting go. The fanana brought its huge head low and uppercutted Casey, knocking her to the ground. The grey beast loomed over her as Casey twisted up to meet it. Cooper stood beside her, head low, waiting for an opportunity to join the melee. Lucky had taken off, along with most of the other animals. Frozen with disbelief, a few small dogs remained.

The fanana lunged, twice snapping at Casey but closing only on air. Casey slowly circled the massive animal, droning on with a deep warning growl. With expert quickness, the beast lunged suddenly, knocking Casey back. She yelped as her back left hind paw twisted in the ground. As she tried to get up, the grey animal pinned her to the ground, and opened its jaws to deliver a deep and fatal bite. The jaws dove, seeking their mark.

A ball of golden fur crashed through Casey's field of vision, knocking the fanana to the ground. Casey struggled to her feet as a wild and angry Cooper sank his jaws deep into the fanana's neck. The fanana let out a choked howl.

Casey whirled to her feet and saw three more fananas coming to the rescue. "Quickly Cooper, we have to get out of here! More of these mammoths will be here in a half second!"

Casey ran, feeling the twinge in her paw. Her legs carried her quickly through the hole in the side wooden fence. She emerged into the dark street of the eerily quiet neighborhood. Cooper was right behind her as she ran.

"Cooper, we have got to enact an emergency meeting upon our return. These have got to be dealt with," she barked breathlessly. She looked back, and far behind them, four fananas howled in pursuit. They were definitely gaining in small increments. Casey considered her own stamina in what would surely be a long distance to run.

"Casey," Cooper barked, "we're in trouble." And they ran, and Casey knew it to be true.

SUBMISSIVIST STRATEGY

Nighttime. Juniper sat atop the ravine overlooking his subdivision. Three other small dogs flanked him: a burly Scottish Terrier named Rip, a Westie named Gorman, and an Italian Greyhound. His humans called him "Tippy," but he was referred to as "Early" by the local lobbyists and staff of the various senators in the Central Canine Government. He was notorious for telling everyone that they should have come or sent a scentima over "earlier" if they wanted a private audience with Juniper. Early was at once Juniper's echo and chew toy, as it was he who bore the brunt of the punishment for all of Juniper's failings. Several years ago, when Juniper had sought the President's office, there had been a debate for which Juniper was poorly prepped. Widely rumored that it had been due to his failing to focus on internal issues over trans-species' issues, which were prominent at the time, Juniper had focused his vitriol on Early. The angst and bitterness that he engendered in the small, durable canine was transmitted directly to those that sought Juniper's counsel, aid, and advice.

The small hilltop where the dogs sat was alive with the buzz of nocturnal insects, and the darkness was only broken by the moonlight through the clouds. A swarm of fireflies had broken ranks from a nearby bush and flitted about just at the periphery of Juniper's gaze. Juniper sat on his haunches and gazed intently into the distance, focusing on nothing in particular. The subdivision over which he stood was comprised of big, illustrious houses. It was a typical neighborhood in the East-town area, the most heavily Submissivist region in the Central Canine Government. The three canine aides sat behind him. These nocturnal meetings were a typical monthly occurrence, but were usually brief and adjourned with the onset of darkness. This time, however, Juniper's aides had waited for over an hour until Juniper padded in late, disgusted. He said nothing. The fireflies finally caught his attention and broke his reverie.

"Boys," Juniper addressed them, en masse, as usual, "do you see the fireflies over there?"

Rip opened his mouth to reply, but Early preemptively shot him a glance, warning that the question was rhetorical.

"The public is very much like the fireflies. Randomly scattered, without any seeming purpose. A select few may sometimes appear to have some semblance of goals, but they are predominantly a purposeless mess."

"Senator, sir, every day we battle such—"

Juniper interrupted Early's sycophantic reply. "Sometimes, fireflies must deal with emergencies. I once noticed what happened as smoke from a nearby fire encroached upon their territory. They lined up, bunched up I guess more than a true line, but clearly formed a cohesive unit, and managed to get themselves out of harm's way. That fire was terrible and caused dozens of dogs in a big apartment complex to be homeless, but I was too engrossed in this fascinating behavior. Those little, silly fireflies, with nary a brain cell in their tiny heads to direct any degree of sophisticated actions, were organized enough to generate a fear-driven response."

"I'm not sure we follow what you mean, Senator," Early offered. "I feel we have been strong advocates, pushing for planning against the Wilds to hopefully avoid such conflicts."

Juniper let out a condescending snort. "Well, Tippy, we have focused on such things, but my observation of these lowly insects has led to other such revelations about our purpose and the direction that *this* government needs, on the Wilds, and elsewhere."

"Well, what do you mean? Should we..."

Juniper readjusted his sitting position for emphasis, even turning a bit to direct his attention to Early and the other two. "It was the ants that finally sealed it up for me. For weeks after the fire, I was obsessed with the fireflies. I would devour my food even faster than usual so as not to miss dusk when they emerged. I tried and watched and watched and not again did I see that beautiful cohesiveness again. I was musing over it in my lawn when I dug up an entire colony of ants at the edge of my yard. I had been angry and did it out of spite, but, as I was finishing, I paused noticing that what had seemed random with them, as well, now turned into a clear directive-based ballet of insect movements."

"Why do you feel this has bearing with the issues with the Wilds?"

"The Wilds this!! The Wilds that!!" Juniper growled, turning on the others, who instinctively cowered. "We jockey back and forth on this, but what have we accomplished?! I toiled for years before I ran for the highest office in our canine government, and the polls said it to me again and again: nothing done, nothing accomplished. You know that not to be true! The tons of information we've had to filter, the threats we've had to head off before they actually became news, so *much* done, but that was not the perception. Do you know why?!"

Early fully sprung up from his cowered stance, obsequious contempt smeared across his muzzle, "Because they're fireflies."

"That's right! Fireflies! They flit about and you can wave at them, run through them, bark at them, and they just re-organize into some other chaotic formation. Nothing done, nothing accomplished. I have fought and fought to prevent war, but not one daft Dachshund or lousy Labrador notices a non-event. Gentlepups, it's the days that it rains, and not the ones that it doesn't, that stick in your mind. That's why my observations of the ants were so telling and important. When I saw the reaction after disrupting one ant pile, I had to see what would happen on a larger scale. In one of the corners of our beloved dog park, hub of our governmental activities and a huge social arena, there is an area covered in ants and littered with their perfect little, symmetric mounds. In between official government business barely a few weeks past now, I laid in watch, attention completely focused on the goings-on of the ants. Sure, there were occasional lines and clumps of them, but they were chaotic and diffusely scattered. Various times of the day, different weather conditions: nothing seemed to matter. I could make not snouts or tails of it all. When I felt sufficiently satisfied that I knew the ants, knew their social superstructure, or lack thereof more appropriately, I cruelly tore into their neat little piles, dug up their tunnels which you barely make out, although I could certainly make out their distinctive scentimic pattern. I dug their cozy little community up four to six paws deep."

Early, sufficiently intrigued and drawn in by Juniper's enthusiasm, whimpered, "Senator, what happened then?"

Juniper sniffed, mouth seeming to curl into just a slight smile, and nearly coquettishly looked down at Early, "Nothing. At first. Unlike the firefly dance, there was even greater disorder. No clear coordination. No impressive rank-and-file tactics. I trotted away."

Juniper paused, licking his snout as if some morsel remained along the rim of his muzzle, so satisfied, he continued, "When I came back barely a half day following, I was initially even more disappointed until I noticed that the ants had split into three communities, although apparently interlinked to some degree as some ants would cross back and forth, but where there clearly had been a central conglomeration of these insects, now there were three busy little central areas. Not only that, but the change in the landscape changed the organization of their mounds. Obviously, I cannot begin to know their minds, but they seemed just as content, just as efficient, and just as beautifully and ignorantly disorganized."

Early and the two other pups exchanged confused glances. Rip barked the obvious, "So what of them, Senator?"

Juniper licked his muzzle thoughtfully. "A short while ago, one of the representatives who works for the Committee of Governmental Regulations and Education reminded me of Section thirteen of the Canine Constitution. He had been consulting the Reciting Barkers regarding obscure laws that were up for review.[9] Section thirteen is a long article, full of a lot of 'what-ifs' should there be sickness or disappearance of key governmental officials and the protocols for replacement and/or re-election. However, this particular representative, Bailey, I believe her name was, had said it reminded her of the tri-dogverate section, wherein, if a simple majority of the district representatives give a vote of no confidence in the

9 At this time, canine society relied solely on a verbal historical record. A group of incessantly barking dogs were nearly constantly reciting key passages of the Canine Constitution. They were the keepers of the information, but it often needed to be pruned down and forced some older legislation to be lost over time.

current government at a time of crisis, the president is automatically removed from office, and there is a tri-dogverate leadership immediately placed into power, composed of the three most powerful committee heads. That includes the Committee for Defense. Furthermore, the tri-dogverate law states that no election will take place. All executive decisions require a best of three majority. If such a thing were to happen now, the other two parts of the tri-dogverate would be Kelly, who is a waffling dolt on the Committee of Canine Health, and Reese from the Committee of Human Endearment, who would never think to subvert me. With those two, I'd be able to do anything I pleased." Juniper turned to lord over the other three, barking for emphasis on the important pieces of information. Early wagged his tail reflexively.

"So," yipped Early, "what do you need us to do?"

Juniper's muzzle stretched into a thin smile. "What do most Submissivists want with the Wilds, what do they feel will resolve everything?"

"War, sir,"

"Exactly. Do what you need to do. Create misinformation. Whatever cables you receive, make sure that only one out of every three is relayed. With a breakdown in communication, it's only a matter of time before we start to get some skittishness on the borders with the Wilds. As every military dog and canine police force member knows, it has taken all of my life's energy to evade war. Without constant attention, things will start to erode."

A thought struck Gorman, who had a knack for sticking his paw in his mouth, "But Senator Juniper sir, if we have a war, how do we avoid another Big Cull?"

Juniper was silent. He was born long after the last war, but the legends were handed down through generations. For years, the conflict had been building between the Wilds and the "civilized" canines. Each had solace in their respective communities, the Wilds ran free in a concrete environment relying upon the business and bustle of the surrounding human-mates for survival. If the human-mates did not notice them, they could function as they pleased. The dogs of the Central Canine Government preferred the safety and security of the houses of their human-mates. When the fighting broke out, there were casualties on both sides. This attracted the human-mates' attention, and they rounded up hundreds of dogs for extermination. Both sides blamed the other when an uneasy truce was called. The specter of another Big Cull was a deterrent, but memories of it faded over time.

Juniper shook off the horrific thought and ignored the small aide's question.

Juniper turned to look at the subdivision before continuing, "Ok, let's get down to more trivial matters and go over the minutes from this last week's meeting again."

Gorman's thought had made Rip think about past crises. "Remember when the Squirrel Incident Report was interrupted? Now that was a mess..."

Juniper caught the last half of it. "That's right...interesting..." he thought to himself.

Far off, a howl was sent off unlike those previously heard. The two aides heard it and looked wide-eyed at Juniper, but he was too absorbed in his own plans to notice. With only one ghostly howl, they soon forgot.

PRECARIOUS PROPOSAL

The canine President Darma, a stout German Shepherd female, barked sharply and methodically in order to get all the committee members in appropriate position before presenting the topic of the Senate meeting.

Chuckles could hear her and caught snippets. "Can we start? Do we have mostly everyone? Honestly, I don't know why I met such resistance to calling this a Level One...I know, I know it's an odd occurrence...Why do you think I called it?" Sasha waited patiently as the other dogs got themselves in order.

Chuckles and Sasha were the representatives of their committee while Casey and Cooper were in West-town. There were three levels to the urgency of the meetings, differentiated by attendance requirements. Level One meetings required attendance. This, a Level Two meeting, required attendance from two or more members on each committee. Chuckles, the inherent pessimist who could not be bothered with the "trappings" of a government of which he was a contributory cog, was nevertheless intrigued by the seeming urgency of today's meeting.

"It seems, Sasha, that we continue to get bombarded with strange occurrences. Do you know what today's meeting is about? Sasha?"

Sasha peered across the dog park enclave at Juniper and his lackeys.

"Sasha?" Chuckles persisted as he paused in his inquiry of her to bite a fly that kept on nibbling at his left ear. Darn it! These flies seemed to have a discriminatory stance against small dogs. He could not remember the last time Casey or Sasha snapped at a fly.

Sasha interrupted his self-deprecating thoughts, "When was the last time *all* of the defense committee attended a Level Two meeting? Even Buck is with Juniper. Buck! He has barely moved from his porch since Juniper started to dominate the defense agenda. It's odd. What's this meeting about, anyway?"

Chuckles turned to a junior Dalmatian senator from the Committee of Canine Health, whom he recognized by sight from prior meetings. "Say, Senator Dalmatian...," Chuckles paused trying to pull the name from his memory.

"Lindie," the Dalmatian replied, "The name is Lindie, sir."

The Dalmatian was so good-natured with his response that Chuckles was taken aback. Despite being a three-term senator and feared from a policy standpoint by several other more senior senators, Chuckles always felt he was put aside in most interactions because of his size. "Well...uhhh...just wondering what the topic was, as all I got from the bees was that it was a 'semi-urgent Level Two' meeting. That, well, that was the first I've heard of such a qualifier for any meeting in years."

"Hmmm, I just got that it was a Level Two. Maybe your messenger bees are learning to editorialize a bit. Anyways, the topic is a introductory investigation into the movement of the Squirrel Incident Report. They just picked up and moved the entire operation seemingly without warning."

"It's never in the *same* tree," Sasha chimed in. "That whole patch of trees is so expansive. Sometimes it takes us half a day to find them even though they are far from silent when they get going."

"No, no, no, Husky Senator Ma'am. It moved an entire district to a patch of trees one quarter the size of their usual location."

Chuckles and Sasha paused trying to absorb the gravity of the situation. "Well, what could possibly motivate the squirrels to do so?"

"Why do you think we're here?" responded Lindie rhetorically. He then padded off to the rest of his canine pals with the Committee of Health.

Chuckles looked up in time to see President Darma finish reciting the statement of loyalty. "...And allow carambee to guide us in our actions, our loyalties, and our dreams and goals.[10] Junior and senior

---

10 Darma was likely reciting, as was the custom of that time, the Canine Unity Declaration. A brief statement aimed to remind all canines what the aim of government was. At this time in history, the Contrarians were deeply opposed to its required usage, as it was thought to imply a reference to an outdated mode of thinking although the notion of carambee was a guiding principle for both parties.

Senators, canine ladies and gentlemen. I have, in accordance with Section 7, Article 4a, called this meeting to set forth in motion the best next course of action to a sudden change in our inter-species communication. I kept the details of the agenda hidden because I did not want bias brought to the bowl before our discussion, but, no doubt as with most matters, initial details have emerged. I am here merely to present the initial facts and guide the discussion. From the Committee for Inter-Species Communication, I received some new information and would like to get this single point across: a decision needs to be made today that leads to more answers than questions." President Darma paused and raised her snout briefly to survey the crowd. Chuckles saw what appeared to be a shared glance between her and Juniper. The Beagle stood like a guard dog at his station. Chuckles did laugh to himself a bit though when he noticed that Buck looked ready to fall asleep. His loyalties to his government brought him here, but his Contrarian tendencies kept his mind elsewhere. Buck was a conundrum because his defense policies bridged tastes from the Contrarian and Submissivist camps, but he was staunchly Contrarian when it came to political posturing, as if the loyalty to the party was equivalent to his love for his human-mates.

Darma continued, "Fact number one: The squirrels engaged in the Squirrel Incident Report moved operations midday, without provocation, to a much smaller area of trees in the area just south of here known as Park Haven. Park Haven is traditionally a quiet area for us and gets a lot of puppy support because of its high human loyalty: canine ratio. Except for its position being not closer or farther from the center of the Wilds' main concentration of population and force, there is nothing exceptionally remarkable about the movement except that it was always widely thought that the squirrels preferred a larger area. Fact number two: No human endeavors have been noted in conjunction with their movement. Fact number three: The order of the acorn readings has completely reversed. Traditionally, the order has been a health and environmental status report followed by puppy observation and enrollment report, followed by several military reports with the last set of reports being variable cross-species inputs. Now, the cross-species input reports are definitely first followed in reverse order. We know this because it took several days for us to sort out conflicting signals and reports before we realized that we were looking at the wrong messages. Fact number four: Despite the nature of the messages across disciplines not being different, the volume of the reports has quadrupled. We have no information to explain this phenomenon, but I have been overseeing this committee for four years, and there is a deeper significance that we do not yet have our snout on. I will now open up this matter to the floor for any questions, and then we will go committee by committee to form an action plan."

The Squirrel Incident Report was a fantastic resource for the canines. Years ago, when the canines were starting to organize into coalitions and found commonalities between groups, a group of Bloodhounds came across a trove of acorns. Although scentimas left along various paths virtually guided any dog in a desired direction, the Bloodhounds found an incredible concentration of scentimas embedded within the pattern on the acorns scored by the squirrels' teeth. Through trial and error, they verified the information contained in the acorns and found that the squirrels had a definitive pattern: they relayed the information in a reliable and ordered fashion every day. With coordinated and verifiable information, dogs could be better mobilized across the burgeoning government's territory. Indeed, the blossoming of the size and structure of the government mirrored the level of utilization of the Squirrel Incident Report. No canine knew why they reported the information so reliably and predictably, but no canine questioned a system that never broke. Every canine in the room felt that this unexplained movement, which left even the brightest dogs baffled, was an unpleasant and foreboding sign of things to come.

A senior committee member on the Committee of Health, a meticulous Doberman named Dante, broke the silence. "The real question, Madame President Darma, is what impact, if any, does this have on our regular affairs? Because we are unable to understand the mechanism behind their movements, we declare it an emergency? What do I care what the squirrels do between their times of chronicling our reports? If I were to move my resting place in my yard to the other side, would it matter to you or to canine-dom as a whole? How come I feel you are taking an alarmist stance to provoke us into action, which by the end of the meeting will be conflict, and in a week will be war."

Only a few of the Submissivist pooches, to which party Dante belonged, yipped and barked in support. Darma, sitting after her initial statement, stood and padded forward a few feet, and her no-nonsense gaze to the others was enough to quiet the ensemble.

Juniper stood up, ears stiff, "Honorable Senator Doberman-Dante, please understand that I... that is, *we* have studied the movements of the Wilds for the last several weeks. We have received countless scentimas showing shifting movements that have not been seen for years, and, although the movement of the squirrels is not anywhere closer or farther from the main focus of our foul, terrible enemies, I cannot surrender with paws all raised that the squirrels did not move in response to this threat. The reason for their movement may elude us, but I beg of you not to take it lightly, as it may be too late when the actual reason for their movements becomes obvious. Now, I bark too long, and I do have a question for you, President Darma, are their numbers depleted in any way?"

"We know that the census of squirrels per tree remains the same, and they occupy the same number of trees as they always do, and, by that calculation, it appears their numbers are no different."

"I see," said Juniper, pausing for a time that Sasha and Chuckles could swear was planned. "Maybe we need to back-communicate with them."

A hush fell over the other canines amid a trailing whimper of disapproval. The squirrels were the source of all the information, other than scentimas, that the canines used to run their extensive government, but there was never any actual communication with the squirrels. Indeed, most thought the squirrels were simpler crea-tures and were thoughtlessly emptying their brains of the observed events of the world. Not only that, but six years prior, Juniper had headed an expedition in attempts to "recruit" the squirrels to their side as spies against the Wilds. The result had been total disruption of the Squirrel Incident Report, and the term "back-communicate" was synonymous with that incident. The squirrels, for an unknown reason, reacted violently to the attempted communication, which was escalated when Juniper swiped a non-marked acorn before the squirrel brought it up to its tree. Juniper himself had received three gashes, and he survived politically only because the squirrels resumed regular functioning within a couple of weeks. Those weeks, however, were dubbed The Great Canine Divide, and hundreds of canines went missing over that time period, presumably because of the failure to monitor the movements of the Wilds. Not long after, the Bulldog Police force was beefed up considerably and was always ready for deployment should such an incident reoccur. It never did. No other dog dared.

"You disrupted our key information supply once already, Juniper, and you presume to want to do so again?"

"Well," barked Juniper, "we only have questions, and we have no answers. What do we know of squirrels, really? How are we to presume to comprehend the nature of animals when we don't even know how it is they compose their reports. We know they *do* it. We use the information, but our knowledge only paws at the surface of this whole affair."

"Even the idea …," Darma barked and treaded towards the general direction of Juniper, although still a few feet away.

"He makes a decent point, Madame President," a junior representative chimed in. "We are responsible for puppy allotment, and a better understanding of the squirrels would certainly aid our dispersal. Perhaps, just perhaps, back-communication should be sniffed at again."

A general barking erupted from all corners of the enclave. Various points of view could be teased out among the canines. "Sure, sure, leave us blind again and hundreds more will go missing … It is not for us to question the squirrels but be thankful for the knowledge they provide … When, since when, has a squirrel report defined our policies … we answer to them … they likely think they own us … re-establishing canine dominance would be a good thing." On and on the mini-discussions went through the crowd as ripples of doubt and support emerged and solidified.

"I don't believe what I'm hearing," Darma continued. "*I* am the President of the Central Canine Government. I have more experience and a better understanding of cross-species culture then any of you. If such a notion had ever seemed appropriate, I assure you, we would have engaged them in such a way. It is a time of *great* unrest, and a risk too much to take."

Juniper took a breath in anticipation of a vociferous and protracted bark when the burly, weathered Senator Sheepdog-Buck practically stepped on him to take the floor. Juniper closed his muzzle, and the entire room turned to look and listen. "For years I have been the major Contrarian voice on the Committee for Defense, which," Buck's eyes swept over the crowd and met many individually, "has not been easy in light of the…the…exuberance of Juniper. The Submissivists rush to action with the Wilds, while I have vehemently opposed such action because canines would die and puppies would go unloved or even homeless. As Contrarians, we are the majority party now, and we have the moderate voice, and I have cherished and loved our position in this world. Juniper rushes to back-communicate because he thinks it may provide him an edge in a war with the Wilds. I support back-communication because I believe the key to solving the Wilds problem is *not* to engage in such barbaric pursuits. Madame President German Shepherd-Darma, you are honorable, and you embody carambee moreso than most, but you come here with very little information at a time when we need information. Even my strong-minded Contrarian ways cannot deny the urgency of the matters with the Wilds, and soon Juniper, who knows I bark plainly in all matters, will have the votes for a declaration of war at the committee level. He certainly will get enough Submissivist votes in the rest of the Senate despite Contrarians holding key spots on several committees. I tell you and beg you humbly to bring back-communication to our bowl." The canines sat in quiet reflection as Buck left the floor.

Two bees carrying urgent scentimas landed on Chuckles' nose, and he drank in the information. His little lithe body sprung into action, "Sasha, we need to go. There is trouble and little time to act."Sasha had received the same information from the other bee. "I will alert the Bulldog Police immediately."

AN EMPTY BACKYARD

Casey's back paw burned. Her tongue lolled out to one side, and only the clicking of paw pads could be heard for blocks in any direction. Cooper and Casey did not look at one another out of fear of expending any additional energy that might bring the fananas closer. She shuddered. Already they were a mere half block away, gaining all the time, and occasionally a howl would erupt that sparked gruesome images in Casey's mind. Oh, where were her humans when she needed them? She had a vision where they stood like statues around her, and the fananas ran away, fearful of the enigmatic but powerful humans.

They ran down a foreign side street that was, by Casey's calculation, only a few streets away from their home neighborhood. There was a leaning shed on the side yard of the corner house. She was sure a shortcut existed through one of the back yards that would bring her to the safety of her home. Which yard though, which yard? Like felines, the humans were fiercely territorial and erected fences almost as rapidly as houses. Yet, while the cats lived in relative separation, humans lived in ever closer proximity to one another.

Casey and Cooper were midway down the street; the fananas had not turned the corner yet. She had only a moment to find that one yard to safety. Triple tree? Casey vaguely recalled that an odd triple tree formation in the front yard marked the right home. But where was it? She slowed and saw two homes, one with a triple tree formation. She banked hard towards it, only halfway convinced that she was correct.

Cooper, too tired to whimper, shot her a sideways glance. Casey did not return it. She did not achieve success by doubting herself. If it was the wrong house, then they would have to fight their way out.

They angled and turned and simultaneously braked hard, yipping in frustration. A large, silent fence stood blocking their way.

Casey's paw felt as if it dangled from her leg. They were partially hidden in a narrow corridor between the two homes, and they turned to see if the fananas would follow.

They waited, panting hard. Casey wanted to sit but knew that, if action was required, she was better off in a standing position. Heavy panting was difficult to silence, but they licked their muzzles at intervals, and silence descended in the interim. Their eyes flicked back and forth from the side yard entrance to one another and back. Casey began to rejoice, hoping that the fananas had either lost them, given up out of fatigue, or turned back because of the dense human presence.

She heard nothing, but she saw the grey, gruff coat appear at the entrance to the side yard. The fanana, terribly haggard but barely panting, tilted her head at the pair of senators. The night was overcast, but a sliver of light from nearby homes highlighted the fananas' eyes, and a slow growl erupted from the gape in the jaws. The teeth were fearsome. Everything about the animal was sharp and angular; the triangular head, pointed ears, pale yellow eyes that seemed to pierce the fading twilight.

"Arrogant…," she growled in her unusual accent, "you pathetic *dogs* sit and get sticks and run around like fools, but when *they* sleep and you are alone, all your aaaarrroogance is for nothing, nothing. When we are done, not your own humans will be able to identify you." They blocked the entrance and exit, and Casey hoped that she would black out before the final bite came down. Cooper, shaking as if he were afflicted, moved forward barely a step and emitted a growl that was partially drowned out by the wolves' laughter as they edged closer.

A step forward from the leader, a growl, a belch. Belch? Casey could barely think. Was she hallucinating? Two belches. This time, the four fananas heard it. Grunting accompanied the belches at odd intervals. They were distant, coming closer. A building tidal wave was coming this way towards this tiny side yard. Heavy paw padding echoed between the homes on the street, and Casey spotted a lone Bulldog tramping down the slim side street towards the ruckus. One by one, more fell into step behind him. A fourth, fifth. At twenty, Casey stopped counting.

A large, impenetrable semicircle of Bulldogs fearlessly stood a few feet from the fananas, who had instinctively huddled together, teeth and snouts facing outwards towards the greater threat. An occasional belch and grunt could be heard, but, largely, the Bulldogs were now surprisingly quiet, waiting for orders. At the moment where Casey could feel that the lead Bulldog was about to bark his orders, the lead fanana female drowned him out with a laugh and a growl. "This is your civilization?!? Ha! Squat and asymmetric?! The more we see your so-called advances, the more we are shocked at your ineptitude. Warsaw, dispatch a few of these and the rest will scatter." Warsaw leapt forward, teeth bared and snarling.

A blur of white and tan and brindle fur descended upon the fanana, who found he could do little damage to the Bulldogs' formidable skulls. He had little space to get at their forelegs or hindquarters, and he was not nearly quick enough to react simultaneously to the half dozen angry Bulldogs bent on establishing martial law. Three of his ample but vulnerable, narrow legs were soon snapped in half. A ghastly howl went up, and the lead Bulldog shot the lead fanana a half grin.

"Next time, better to let me speak." He harrumphed an order next and Casey turned away before she heard multiple sounds of bones breaking. The fanana lay motionless, his head tilted at an odd angle.

"Care to try again?" The lead Bulldog barked calmly. "By the power given by the canine Congress to substantiate canine law to ensure our natural order, I order you to come with us or suffer the same fate as your … friend, here, or whatever he was."

The silence seemed to last a thousand canine years as the fananas took stock of the situation. Layers of Bulldog Police blocked their exit to the street. The tall wooden fence and the dark, silent house framed them on their flanks. Behind them, two exhausted Retriever senators and a dead end. Casey knew these grey behemoths to be agile, but she knew the nearly seven to eight foot fence behind her was too large for them to leap. The lead fanana peered around herself in all directions. She lowered her head to the Bulldogs, as if about to charge, but instead growled and emitted a few odd whistling sounds. At once the smallest of the pack leapt in a fit of fury at the force.

In the confusion, the lead fanana and her closest cohort leapt over the closest lateral edge of the Bulldog Police contingent. A brief staccato howl erupted from the lead fanana as she bolted away. The Bulldogs, always efficient with energy consumption, watched them go. The smallest pack member lay as his mate, permanently immobilized.

Minutes later, the Bulldogs escorted the two senators home. On the way, the head of the division, an all brindle Bulldog named Wesley, chatted with Casey. "Should I take this as a sign of things to come, Senator? Recruiting may need to be stepped up, you know. There's real power and muscle in those things."

"I do not know what they are or why they seem so like us. But whatever they are, I intend to do a little digging."

"I would suggest the vet first."

Casey noted her own paw. The vet first.

CANINE CONSULTATION

As soon as her human-mates noticed Casey's significant limp, they spirited her to the local veterinary hospital. The hospital was a nondescript, one level brown and white haven for injured canines, felines, and the occasional undomesticated animal. A pristine tiled floor and a front desk too high for most dogs to reach greeted all those who entered the front door. After she was dropped off, Casey was escorted by pleasant and loving human-mates to a long, narrow kennel as she awaited assessment.

What the human-mates did not realize was that the veterinary hospital was a thruway for every canine and feline hustler, lobbyist, and religious zealot. All communications, however, had to go through a mediator, and that role was filled by a slick, one-eyed wanyamas named Jack. Casey sniffed as she thought of him: Jack had traded his self-worth as a feline for this role because he enjoyed the action, often received free food from the humans, and rubbed noses with some of the most elite government officials in the known world.

Casey laid down with her head up, her snout inches from the front of the kennel cage. She could occasionally hear various dogs hawking their agendas, "Reform the puppy deployment system!... Treats for canines, grief for felines: what the Contrarians are not telling you about their hidden agenda!... Love your human-mates, but love your canine roots more!"

Casey was careful not to give off a whimper. She knew it was only a matter of time before word trickled through the kennels and halls of the veterinary hospital that a ranking senator from the Central Canine Government was undergoing treatment.

A small mixed breed Spaniel-Shepherd dog in the kennel adjacent to hers caught her eye. Plywood blockers kept most of the kennels isolated from one another, minimizing the stress of an unlimited view with limited physical interaction that would drive many canines crazy. There was also the occasional militant dog that benefited from the isolation. A triangular chunk was gone from the blocker to Casey's left, however, and she could see a slender black and brown snout lying on the floor. Casey saw an eyebrow twitch and knew the dog to be awake.

Casey flopped on her side, her head flush with the ground and her snout a few centimeters away from the dog. Canines did not achieve public office without a certain sensitivity for suffering friends. "What troubles you, friend?" Casey implored in a gentle canine hum, devoid of all the trappings of official government inter-action.

The wispy-haired ears pointed forward then away, and a nose inched a bit closer. "You seem fairly intact, Labrador. There are others, very unfortunate ones that can only whimper in pain. They cannot even describe the pain or why they hurt. Did you need to visit the confines of this place for medical reasons, or for some other purpose?"

Instantly, Casey knew that she liked this odd mutt. She managed a laugh and continued, "I am injured, but I am also seeking information. I think my paw may need attention, but I am positive it isn't too serious. Have you been here long?"

"Longer than most, but not as long as Jack. What kind of information do you seek? Are you looking for something that has answers or something that will lead you to more questions?"

"I wish I knew. A few weeks ago, I would have given you an assurance that I only need answers, but, in the light of recent issues, questions may be more important." Casey sniffed, "I am interested in seeing what kind of information Jack can bring to me."

A short burst of laughter, "Information is one thing that Jack does not have an abundance of. He's got plenty of innuendos, rumors, hints, and propaganda, but real information may be hard to come by. I would keep my snout up if I were you, random scen-timas in this place may yield you more information."

"For one of its inhabitants, you seem particularly well-informed. Perhaps I should ask you."

"I doubt you would find what I know to be very interesting."

Casey paused and turned things over in her mind. Until that

moment, she had been certain this was a wounded member of the surrounding canine community, but now she doubted whether this canine could be trusted. He seemed odd and strangely detached, although all this could be attributed to his incarceration. She decided to proceed, but paw lightly around the discussion.

"What are you here for?"

"I am a donor, like Jack. However, unlike Jack, I do not have free reign. I am well fed, and I run around several times a day, but talk of freedom from the Submissivists really makes me wonder who the government is really defending. I have talked with many representatives and aides to the main legislative body, but the Contrarians are fools when they talk of adapting our behaviors to endear ourselves further when they do not even know the true nature of our human-mates. None of the talk seems to matter to me. I am an endless observer of a show in which I cannot take part."

"We all have our role. Our human-mates have asked a great sacrifice of you, don't you see that you have likely given life to many of our pups?"

"The only real life is the life of the Wilds; only they are truly free."

Casey nodded, slowly and with understanding. The pooch had been radicalized. Casey had suspected that he was either in pain or crazy: it appeared to be a bit of both.

"I am not sure that you understand the real structure of the world outside of this place, friend," she said, as gently as she could. "The life of the Wilds is a gruesome, sad life, and is not one to envy. Perhaps you have been listening too much to the canines who have poisoned you into thinking that the government is the enemy."

There was a definite pause as the gentle Spaniel mix sighed. His voice dropped into a low, contemptuous register. "Listen to the scentimas come in for you, Senator. I can smell the stench of groveling on each one. The only thing that a government official can definitely guarantee is the necessity of government. I assure you, the Wilds life is one of uncertainty, but that is the cost of true freedom."

Casey sniffed and, sure enough, smelled the scentimas coming in, one after another. The secret was out: they knew she was here.

Dear Most Honorable Senator Labrador:

We at the Canine Centrist Organization, the CCO, want to thank you for your recent efforts in ensuring the puppy deployment system not be changed to a dreaded lottery. It is only through guided deployment that we can ensure that canine interests be truly reflected in all our efforts. Now, however, we once again call you to hear our pleas. The Submissivists have always tried to claim that human loyalty is not fickle if only we stay true to our canine roots, but with all sort of breeds, cross-breeds, and sizes of dogs, how can they claim to know the nature of the true roots of dogs. Furthermore...

"Well, well, well... there is a puppy trapped in a cage of mine, and she is a most honorable and important puppy. Senator Labrador, you have most certainly come to the correct place, if, in fact, you are looking for answers to some dire questions." The voice was one of an oily black and grey feline. He slithered as sleekly as his voice, and his paws padded without a sound. Casey thought of the grey behemoths that chased her and Cooper just a short while ago.

"Well, Jack, your reputation precedes you, but this queer canine to the side of me is not impressed with anything you've had to offer, although he also thinks that the Wilds are to be envied."

"His name is Bruno, and he is my canine counterpart for the hospital here. He loathes his position while I revel in it, but he is a bit of a liar. You see, every few days, he is let out, and the yard in the back has several very large holes, even big enough for your chunky behind. He can easily slip out and join his kind, but he knows nothing of anyone's ways and he knows it."

"I am waiting for the right consort, that is all, feline. You know not of true canine nature. We are waiting for something great for which to reveal our calling to lead the world into a new order, one that maybe does not shackle us to humans." The black, wispy-haired canine stared back and forth at Casey and Jack with intense, gentle eyes.

Jack held back a snicker. "To business, Senator: two rather pushy pups have begged me to tell you that the puppy deployment system is in danger in far West-town, but they will not say more."

"Likely because of a rather unusual problem they've been having."

"By problem, you mean the Originals?"

Casey cocked her head, annoyed that the feline was toying with her. The cat clearly thought it funny to imply that those beasts were superior. She curled her lip. "Listen, you ragged furry ..."

"Before you start barking insults, maybe you should listen to the Council. We're having a rather interesting discussion about recent developments."

"Have anyone interesting in there?"

"Only the oldest functional cat in East-town."

"Murray?" Casey sat up. This must be serious.

"Do you want to hear what he has to say? The other Council members are purring with delight. Everyone is enthusiastic about the upcoming scuffle."

"Why?"

"Because though we may be less organized, we know what will happen and are more resilient than your fragile species."

"Spare me the dramatics. Just open the latch."

Jack backed up a few feet and crouched until his neck appeared to melt into his body. Leaping silently and flicking his front paw upwards midflight, a metal clang sounded, and the cage door swung open. Casey nosed it further, and she ticked her way behind Jack.

A row of five-by-five cages were stacked, and the cats all lounged in various positions. The Council was made up of cats that achieved their position through human neglect. Often, these cats were boarded more than they were home. Always individualistic, they conglomerated into a makeshift group called "The Council" in an effort to provide a semblance of direction to a largely disinterested group. By convention, twenty of the cats were "regulars" and another five were random members of the community that happened to be sheltered in the hospital at the time. There was no interpretation of their charter that allowed for a real leader of the feline community, but, and again by convention, the longest tenured feline boarded at the hospital was the leader. The caveat of this was that the cat had to be "functional": any sign of sickness or illness automatically dispelled that cat from the role. As there were always several cats with five to eight years of kenneling under their collar, there was always a replacement in the wings. This focus on seniority made no sense to Casey, as it seemed, to Casey, to lead to apathy and an overly conservative approach to most problems. "No wonder our numbers always outpace theirs," thought Casey to herself, "we are always changing, evolving to enlarge our role with the human-mates where the felines are only stagnant." Prior to Murray, a particularly ornery cat named Rachel presided over the Council for more than two years. She was black in color, and the canines used to believe that her black coat was darker than any of the other black cats, if only because it reflected the color of her beliefs: dark, void of hope and optimism. Casey encountered Rachel once in her last month and knew that her toughness was largely unequaled among felines.

Now, Murray sat atop the pile. Not one for rules and regulations, he was fairly young, only ten, more verbose than effective.

"Casey...," he hissed and spat the name, "You have caught us at an impasse. Whom do we welcome after the building fray? The new or old oppressors?"

"I don't know what you're getting at. I think we're far from war."

"Then you are already out of touch," Murray roared back.

"She doesn't know—" laughed a calico cat lounging on its back.

"She's a dense pup," chimed in another.

"Let's hear what she has to say. I motion to let the pup have the floor."

"Seconded."

"All right, Retriever-Senator," a particularly brusque feline named Larry mewed, "or Senator-Retriever, or Lord Dogness, whichever you like or seem to prefer. You may speak." Casey's snout squared and her eyes darted from cage to cage. Practically anarchic, the cats barely acknowledged one another before adding their thoughts. Each had total disregard for the others, and each cat felt their word to be the most important. Often, it was hard to catch what was said over the din of seven to eight comments.

"She has no control, I think she's a junior senator. She even—"

"Of course control is the key point, but the dogs can't concentrate it into the correct hands—"

"The Wilds are getting ready—"

"Of course the Wilds are involved, but the key point is what Juniper will—"

"Achieve?? What left is there for us to do but achieve victory when Juniper—"

"Juniper barks as if he knows—"

"The Originals know that he knows—"

"I can't believe she doesn't know—"

"She has no real authority—"

"The Wilds are the ones with the authority, or maybe it's the Originals—"

"ENOUGH!" barked Casey, "I am the senior senator on the Inter-Canine Committee, and my authority is real. And what I know is that you might be better off with us than without us. You think the Wilds respect boundaries??! It is precisely the lack of respect for boundaries that has created this endless threat of war. At least we canines are willing to represent each dog and pup fairly and honestly. The same cannot be said for canines that choose to live by claw and tooth. If you want to gamble with your fur, then go ahead, but I thought most cats were smarter than that."

Casey sat on her hind legs and stared with Labrador intensity at the felines. Every set of cat's eyes penetrated into Casey's face as she finished her last point. There was a pause, then...

Yowling and howling laughter!! The cats rolled and purred with delight at the senator's admonitions. Only Murray lay silent, flicking his tail metronomically to one side, then another, giving a gentle yawn.

"Felines," Murray meowed after a further minute of guffawing, "we convene for the purpose of advancing our agenda. Most of the time, we choose to react to what is given to us. Our patience has been our ally but, sometimes, a feline needs to pounce when either prey or enemy is close by. Perhaps, just perhaps, this canine is correct that both civilized canine and feline goals are the same... at least in the short term."

The boldest of the other cats, a feline with a longer snout than most with a deep grey coat stopped her snickering long enough to add, "Murray, sweet leader, we rightly mock the agendas of the dogs. How often do we hear a 'key' lobbyist of the canines come to us and beg for support to bring his or her canine issue to the forefront of canine politics. It's all the same. Today, this crisis cannot wait. Tomorrow, that crisis is a distraction. If the dog wants to convince us of a 'reality,' then she and the rest of them need to make up their minds on what that reality is. We are indifferent, but consistently so."

This time, hisses erupted with the laughter, signifying the Council's distaste for the dogs. Casey noticed that several of the felines pawed at the air playfully, as if batting away the senator's concerns.

Casey's hair stood to outline her spine, "I don't need you," she said, her voice calm. She yawned slowly and closed her mouth with a forceful snap. "I'll figure out what the crow meant in due time."

Casey padded away. At the door, she cast a brief glance at the cages. All of the felines leaned forward, eyeing her intently. With a shrug, she turned away and nosed the door open. A sharp meow cut the silence.

"Senator Labrador-Casey," mewed one of the felines, "did you just say 'crow'?"

A sneeze then a slight snicker. They wanted to have more fun with her. "Yes, and I suppose you'll tell me next how little you care."

Murray sat back on his haunches and drew up to his full height, looking as regal as a cat named Murray could look. "Senator Labrador-Casey," he intoned, "the birds are the ones who sanction a lot of what we do. It is our feline belief that the rule of the skies supersedes that of any on the ground. We attribute many of the wrongs in our world to the whims of the birds. They can go anywhere. They are not bound to any humans and they are as fast as the fastest animal on land. We know only pieces of some of their language, but no feline has ever been successful in engaging any of the birds."

Casey studied the other cages, looking for the put-on. The cats were silent. She drew her ears out reflexively, searching for any stray flicker of noise that they might let slip. Only a slight rush of air hit her ears. Not even a tail swished across the back of the cages.

"First, I find that ridiculous. You obviously don't know the power of our human-mates. Second, this crow, or the one I thought to be a crow, spoke bits of our language, Domesticated Common.[11] It was trying to warn me, I think, in regards to something about West-town."

Murray's eyes opened wide, stunned. Casey cocked her head and sniffed at him. After a few long moments, he blinked and shook his head. "This is odd, Senator Casey, but I think it is vital." He leaned forward, ingratiatingly. "What, exactly, did the crow say to you?"

Casey sniffed. "You think that I'll give you information after you insulted me by referring to the fananas as the Originals?"

A feline stirred, and Murray meowed angrily for him to keep still. Now, there was order! Murray purred, standing, "A sort of joke, Senator, and a sort of religious fervor among the more docile of us. Most like me find it amusing that some of the more radical cats talk of times when we were larger, so large that not a pack of dogs would dare bother us."

Casey could not help but laugh. The absurdity of the notion!

"You can laugh, pup, but when we teach our young, we educate them about the basics of life. We do know one thing: many come from one. The fananas must be related to you, and although you think they are savage and primitive, they must surely have come before you."

The hair on Casey's spine fluffed a bit of its own accord. "A squirrel and chipmunk look like one another, but no fool would claim they are of the same kind."

"Nevertheless, Casey, there is a possibility. Part of what makes us efficient hunters, far better than your kind, is our ability to

11 Canines and felines each had their separate language, but there was a mixture of both, called Domesticated Common, at least that's what it loosely translates to, that was shared by both. It was rumored that certain other animals, guinea pigs, hamsters, etc. spoke some of Domesticated Common by picking it up in pet shops and other such places, but that has never been verified.

anticipate many types of situations and see the like and the not-like in the same. Yes, this is part of the religious zealotry that also claims our giant ancestors, but I would not claim to be entirely separate from a large cat if I saw one. Now, you have seen one that is similar in many respects, and for the life of me, I will not claim to be able to understand how a Dachshund could come from one of those fananas, as you call them. Then again, I supposedly have a cousin who is ten times the size of me... and I am a large cat."

Casey eyed Murray and sniffed the others. She slowly went from cage to cage, and, at length, satisfied herself that they were sincere. They believed their own crazy talk. Even Jack sat on his haunches in the corner, listening and ignoring several messenger gnats that brought updates on various demands throughout the hospital. Maybe they did have information.

"So," she said, "what would you like to know about the crow?"

Murray's gaze bored into Casey, almost as if she was prey, "How do you know it was a crow?"

Casey shuffled her paws, tick, tick, on the floor. She didn't, exactly. "It was black—"

Murray meowed sharply, cutting her off. "Do you know how many birds are black or so dark that they might be mistaken for black? Of course, a puppy, even a senator, could not and would not know a crow—"

"There's more kitty! The shape of the beak and the eyes, their focus, I've heard about crows, it all seemed to match—"

The cats erupted again.

"Here the puppy goes—"

"She'll make anything up to please..."

"Well, of course she's just a puppy, senators, congresshounds, they're all the same—"

"And I still don't understand why the human-mates find them so indispensable—"

"Pleasing the humans?! Human-mates don't know—"

"How could they know?"

"WOOOFFFRAAAWWWW!" Casey did her dogged best to imitate the raucous pitch of that bird's call.

The cats were as abrupt in their silence as in their protests once again.

Murray was motionless. "Is that what you heard?" inquired Murray, as calmly as if conversing with his closest feline confidants.

"Yes. That was his call. There was also some Domesticated Common language about West-town."

"Well, Senator Casey, that is the call of a crow. However, even if I tried to let you know the significance of this, I do not believe that I could impress upon you the gravity of the situation. Maybe it is best ... Jack?"

"Yes, sir," meowed the crafty one-eyed feline.

"Take her to Fanatics' Row. The last cage on the left. Senator Casey, you will ask her about the sign of the crow."

Casey turned, and Jack's black and grey tail was already out the swinging door opposite to where she had entered from. One look at the multiple grave faces of the feline Council, and Casey started after her.

"Casey, one more thing," Murray offered.

Casey paused and half-turned her head.

"The other dogs and cats ... they will try to *sell* you their thoughts. They will attempt to convince you that the crow has some meaning in relation to their own worldview."

"So ...?" Casey barked back.

"The others' views are fallacies. Some dogs and even cats have gone mad after visiting the fanatics. I would not stay any longer than necessary."

None of the other cats said otherwise. Casey, anxious and excited, padded after Jack.

PUPPY PERSUASION

"Chuckles, you have done excellent work within committee. The three most recent bills that you have co-authored have advanced the overall canine agenda without being deleterious to our society at large. In addition, your victory over Losha, the glum of a Saint Bernard, was momentous in terms of what it meant for dogs of smaller stature everywhere. Truly, size cannot possibly matter, and you know no one believes it more than myself." Juniper, oozing praise, sat on haunches at the dog park.

"What can I do for you, Senator Juniper?" Chuckles yipped back, leery of this outpouring of praise from the normally stolid Beagle.

"We have reliable canine intelligence that the Wilds are looking to move against us with overwhelming force. Casey and Cooper's aggressive investigation missed the most obviously guilty actors, the Wilds. They detest our way of life. They feel we are immoral and evil, and they will stop at nothing to expose what they see as our hypocrisy."

Chuckles was not easily manipulated, and his mind churned as to why he was being targeted for this covert meeting. Until Juniper exposed his belly, it was likely best to have a civil canine conversation. "That's a big leap, to state that the entire agenda of the Wilds is bent on our destruction, but you're ignoring the obvious dilemma of the canine-like beasts that Casey and Cooper came in contact with."

Juniper yipped in laughter before responding, "Who knows what kind of breeding practices the Wilds entertain? They have no rules. Is it not possible that the Wilds created a subset of warriors within their own ranks to unleash upon us? The Bulldogs, although formidable, are not invincible, and if scores of those thugs invade us as a first wave, we are finished. All that you value in your quiet little neighborhood won't even be a consideration, and survival in the aftermath will be the new reality."

"I'm not one of your voters, Senator Beagle-Juniper," Chuckles barked back. "Scare tactics and conspiracy theories sound odd coming out of the leading member of the Defense Committee."

Juniper sat back to scratch his ear as several flies brought scentimas to him intermittently. They were likely keeping him abreast of key intelligence and defense movements throughout their conversation, Chuckles thought. They came in so regularly, though, that it almost seemed as if Juniper orchestrated them to give the impression that intelligence data flowed constantly. Juniper seemed to pause a moment before changing the tones of his barks. "You are hardly one to talk. The rumors of the means of your re-election have stretched across our committee. Our new candidate that we are marching against you has considerable experience, and you won't be able to play the small dog card to sway the populace."

Chuckles yipped back before Juniper could finish his conjecture, "So, you thought you'd cater to my common canine sense to help you in support of all out war? Am I one of the first you have seen today, signifying my vulnerability, or are you kicking up the dirt at the fence all at once and just seeing which sticks?"

Juniper turned his snout to absorb the abuse, not quite a gesture of submission, but rather one of acknowledgement. "Chuckles, would you trot with me, without any of my aides around? We can bark more frankly."

They walked side by side on the winding path around the perimeter of the dog park.

"The fananas' appearance was interesting to me, Senator Chuckles. I had several aides to my own office investigate the allegations. Representative Lucky, although a low-ranking member in our party, is also quite injudicious in his allegiances, so I thought that he may have brought on the involvement of these animals himself, albeit in some roundabout, difficult-to-trace kind of way. Yet, Lucky has stated, however, that the fananas had never become so aggressive as the day that Casey and Cooper showed up. That is curious and troubling. Do you see the point I am trying to make?"

"Lucky is obviously a fringe representative," Chuckles barked back. "His district having almost no legislative importance. It's not surprising to me that the fananas saw an opportunity to strike at key government members, and they bit off more than they could chew."

"More than that, Senator. The disruption that Casey and Cooper caused by their romp could be seen as a clear violation of the Canine Nonintervention Pact, whereby any canines that instigate violence with the Wilds within the borders of canine communities under the umbrella of our government, without alerting the authorities, can be prosecuted as co-conspirators under our law." Juniper's step almost seemed to lift him higher and higher off the ground as he recited key parts of the law.

Chuckles shook his head. "That law also states that the canines must instigate the violence with known members of the Wilds. In that case, a reasonable canine would have to be able to trace their lineage back to the Wilds directly, or through contacts. How do you propose to trace an animal that has never been seen back to the Wilds?"

"I have sworn statements from Lucky, who is a slime and is likely looking to expand his own political influence, to be sure, but that does not make him a liar as well. Lucky is ready to give sworn testimony that these animals are members of the Wilds. In addition, he has the full support of most members in his district. There is much fear, and they want resolution."

Chuckles pointed his snout towards the ground in apparent reflection, his thoughts racing. Juniper was hinting at a controversial canine law that involved making his and other votes forfeit. Years ago, when the tendrils of the canine government were being established, there were only four main committees: Internal Matters, Puppies' Agenda and Health, External Matters related to Canines, and Canine Oversight and Extra-Species Involvement. Each committee had nine members, the tie-breaking vote going to the party with the predominance of seats. None of the canines at that time were beyond corruption, however, and a bill supporting amnesty for former Wilds members adopted by humans at shelters came up for a vote. Seven of the members on the Committee of External Matters represented districts with massive numbers of former Wilds dogs, all of whom were eager to reap the reward of participation in the fledgling government. The committee members redrew the districts to encompass more than ninety percent of the new citizens, an act illegal on its face. Fortunately, the Committee of Canine Oversight had kept a watchful eye and brought the matter to the attention of the canine president, a tough-as-a-Pit bull Brittany Spaniel named Ruben, who made an emergency speech that prompted indictment of the seven committee members and defeat of the bill. A bill was then passed that stated if the ranking leader of a committee was under official indictment, all votes of that committee were null and void. If the accusing party was within the same committee, however, only the leader lost their vote, and all members retained their voting rights. If Juniper had enough evidence or testimony to accuse Casey, all the votes of their committee would be lost, unless Chuckles participated in the allegations.

"You want me to be a traitor to Casey," Chuckles finally whimpered.

"To be seen to be associated with Casey when the charges become filed would damage you politically. In addition, the Committee for Inter-Canine Communication is the strongest Contrarian committee in our Senate. You would be supporting a dog that may lose her seat due to illegal activities. True, I brought up the infractions to let you know how ready I am to get the votes I need for a full-on indictment, but I know how fragile the Contrarian political stance is right now. You would be best to realize the extent of your influence also. Our intentions are to draw out this investigation through the upcoming elections, and who knows what the outcome will be?"

Chuckles was the only Contrarian on his committee up for re-election, and the rumors circulating around the districts were starting to wear into his healthy support. The Submissivists, currently the minority party, were leveraging the growing unease about recent events into potential votes. And the fananas were a hot topic, despite earnest attempts by the Central Canine Government to minimize the uproar. The idea of large, ruthlessly aggressive dog-like creatures running around the districts was a grave canine security risk. In truth, because the fananas were not officially recognized, they were not being officially monitored either. More junior members within the Contrarian party were pushing the higher-ups to take a stance, any stance, so as to open an investigation into the issue. With elections so close, however, senators like Casey and Sasha were not willing to burn their reserve chew toys when the outcome was not clear. Chuckles was one of the few more senior senators to support greater involvement in the matter, and, ironically, it was he who was facing the tough re-election bid.

"I would lose nearly everything I have dug for by going against Casey," whimpered Chuckles.

"How many times have Casey and Sasha changed their votes for political gain? Three months ago, both of them supported several of my recent bills knowing full well they had deals with other subcommittees to aid measures to kill the bills just so they could appease more moderate members of the Contrarian party. This is part of the political game, Senator, nothing more."

As they trotted along the exterior path, Chuckles worried that other dogs were listening in on their conversation. Most canines at the park were civilians, but he was sure he saw a junior representative on the Committee of Health a few bushes back. It seemed uncharacteristically quiet. Chuckles snorted in frustration, "You'll get a vote of tails-down from me when you submit your charges. I don't want to take part in this messy business."[12]

Juniper's step almost seemed to lighten. "Well, Senator, if I cannot have your support, I will do my best to shield you from any collateral fur that may fly from the coming fray. Be warned, though, that I might not be able to."

Far from the area where the small Dachshund and only slightly larger Beagle trotted side by side, a tiny gnat came crashing back to Sasha's nose. Sasha drank it in. Her eyes steeled. Huskies were notoriously loyal.

---

12 A vote of "tails-down" was equivalent to an abstention. A "paws-up" vote was in favor and "paws-down" vote was against.

FERVOR OF THE OPPRESSED

W here the Council had cats that were barely wanted but always retrieved, the Fanatics' Row was a mixture of both canines and felines that no one wanted. Always on adoption lists, but never adopted, Fanatics' Row consisted of eight cages. Loved by the hospital's staff like personal mascots, the five dogs and three cats were all mainstays, but yearned constantly for freedom. Solaced by their thoughts, each one of the fanatics found a particular following among various subdivisions of the two species, and, in that way, they found their freedom living on through their teachings.

Casey whispered to Jack as she approached the now quiet row, "Are they always this silent?"

"The fanatics have all spent many months dictating their theories to their adjuncts via scentimas. Their main role now is interpretive: where there appears to be a paucity of direction in a given scenario, they can elaborate on how or how not a given action is in line with their teachings."

Casey nodded. The dealings of the Central Canine Government were largely secular, not by design, but more as a reflection of the lack of perceived utility in religious teachings. The vast majority of the canines under government jurisdiction were free more than they were caged, and at that time were defined by their linkage to the human-mates.

Casey stood in front of a massive cage, three times as tall as her. An Irish Wolfhound lay before her, all shaggy and gruff appearing. It seemed to look Casey up and down at the same time. His nearly black eyes were deep and soulful, and his demeanor seemed so empathetic that it seemed to Casey he might weep with her if she asked him nicely.

"What can I do for you, gentle Senator Labrador?"

Casey harrumphed. She remembered Murray's warning, but did not want to be rude. Could dogs really go insane from a few musings from caged pups? Besides, something about the Wolfhound's sheer size drew her near to him as if he could be a father to dozens of puppies. She had to know what this canine wanted to say.

"Well, my dear friend, I'm not sure if you will have any answers for me. I have very complex questions."

"Our beliefs are not concerned with the simplicity or complexity of your problems. The great Donor loves you all the same and can help you with your problems, if you want to let Him."

"I understand that you have powerful beliefs, as they certainly have drawn in many followers, but I am trying to ascertain the meaning of several events, none of which may be related, while also trying to stave off outright war and preventing the more volatile of our political parties from taking control."

"This may be your harness, gentle Senator Labrador."

"My harness?"

"Yes, my dear Senator Labrador," the Wolfhound crawled near to the cage edge, allowing him to continue to speak only to her. "You see, many generations ago, so many that not you and dozens of other dogs with all your paws could count them, the great Donor created a puppy that had the hairs of all the dogs. Each one of his hairs was like that of the purest breeds, and he had hairs for half-breeds and mutts and, in truth, every possible type of dog you could think of. Each one was represented in this puppy. The puppy's hair shone brilliantly but not harshly, beautifully, like the reflection of the setting sun on a lake. The puppy had all the best traits of all the breeds, and he was the helper of the animal kingdom. When the chipmunks could not find their food, the puppy sniffed it out and found it for them. When little birds lost their mother, the puppy could hear so wonderfully and track so well, he could return all the lost little ones to their mothers. All the other animals knew the puppy to be honorable and fine, and they would praise the puppy and tell him how special he was.

"But all that praise and affection was like so many other things in our world. In small and moderate doses, they help you, but in large doses they are poisons. And so it was with the puppy. One day a skunk said to this puppy as he helped her avoid a trap, 'You are the greatest of all the animals, most wonderful puppy, we should be worshipping you as you help more than the great Donor.' Such animals had said this to him many times, and he always replied that it was only through the great Donor that he could do such things. This time, though, the puppy was so puffed up with pride that he agreed and wondered if maybe he was greater than that which created him? The great Donor, wise and knowing so much more than any canine was meant to know, became very sad, because he had endowed the puppy with so many gifts. He thought about chastising the puppy and allowing him to remain as he was. Sadness turned to anger, though, when the great Donor realized the puppy had changed and would truly never again value all that the Donor had bestowed upon him. So, he said to the puppy, 'You are one of my most beautiful of creations, but now you deny the rightful place of Me in relation to you, and so you must be punished.' And he looked down upon and touched the puppy, and the puppy shed all of his hairs. 'Each hair will be a different breed, and your talents and abilities will be diversified among a community of different dogs. Now, none of you can claim superiority over any other dog.' The puppy was ashamed, and he cowered before the great Donor. The great Donor touched him again and said, 'And with every day that passes, you will lose the beauty of a puppy, and you will age and surely die.' Ever since then, we shed and we age, revealing our shame to the great Donor.

"A dark time came upon the canines. Food became scarce, and dogs attacked one another, descending into complete lawlessness. There was no longer any joy in our lives, and we became cruel savages. Many generations passed like this, and dogs barely survived. There was no such thing as carambee towards any other canine. The great Donor saw this and was deeply saddened. He breathed life into another very special canine, a dog that had a paw and a tail that was part of the flesh of the great Donor Himself. This dog knew something that no other canines before him knew and none have known since: he could completely understand the language of the human-mates. This canine, whom we call Sage, told the canines that they must love and respect one another, and that their savagery

would destroy one another. When the food supply had run danger-
ously and finally low, Sage went out on a dark, snowy night and
found the human-mates. They told him that a human-mate was lost
and near death and asked Sage to go and find him. Sage did so and
let the lost human-mate put a harness on him so that Sage could
pull him to safety. Sage pulled and pulled over hundreds of miles,
all in one night, and brought the human to see the dogs. When the
human-mate was finally safe, Sage died, and it was only then that
the dogs knew Sage's words to be true. The dogs helped the human
and the human helped them, and so became the bond between
human and dog. As Sage lay dying he was reported to have said, 'I
accepted the harness not because I needed to, but because I chose to
do so, for you and the humans will together forge a new love bond,
one that will help humans love dogs and dogs love humans, and
which will help dogs love each other, and humans love one another.
Serving someone out of love is why the great Donor, my father, has
made all of you.'"

Casey was sure she had heard some of this before in letters
addressed to her. Whether it was true or not, who could tell? Casey
believed in living in the moment and dealing with issues that canines
had to battle at the time. She could listen for hours to stories about
why the human-mates were so tied to the canine community, but,
in truth, it did not matter to her. It only mattered that it was so
and that she had to operate within its boundaries. The large grey
dog was sweet, but she had a job to do. "Is there anything in your
teachings, or thoughts, or whatever you call it, about the crow?"

"The crow embodies evil and hatred. When only the puppy was
on this land, the crow would steal the grain from plants from which
other animals fed, and the puppy would scare them away. The crow
is a reminder to all of us that when we perform a task, we must be
vigilant, whether it is loving your human-mate or chewing a bone.
Each task must be performed completely and fully, or else someone
else will take our livelihood and eventually our place."

"Our treaty recognizes the sovereignty of the birds. They are no
more evil than we. They rule the skies, and we do not make judg-
ment calls regarding their behavior."

Casey sat with her nose inches from the great dog's cage. At this, he sighed and turned away. Although he appeared dismayed, his strong voice was gentle, "The birds are heathens and recognize no greater power. They are cursed by the great Donor as they can be tossed about by the breeze while we can stay with paws firmly on the ground."

Casey, not accustomed to having any dog, friend or foe, turn their back in disinterest, was about to bark an order at the caged dog to turn and face her when she heard a high pitched laugh that almost sounded feline. She whirled to see a lean, orangish mixed breed dog, who panted heavily. His eyes bored into Casey, and he was amused to the core.

"You're not going to get anywhere with him any longer, Senator. His faith is one of the weak, and he does not yet realize that the true goal of that power in the sky is one of ultimate domination over canines. The crow is an agent of the power that picks and steals the grain as a test of our worthiness."

Casey bounded up and barked into this obnoxious hound, "Enough! I do not care what the crow *represents* to you. I need to know *why* this particular crow came to me, and I need to know how this is linked to what's happening now. Dogs are going missing! Spare me the stories and parables and give me something I can sniff and see."

At that moment, a cowering cat in a cage deeper than the others and farthest down the row interjected into Casey's tirade: "Senator? The crow is a centerpiece of many prophecies. In my teachings, however, it is *the* crucial catalyst."

Casey turned her head to the opposite side, and the orange Greyhound/Ridgeback mix sneered as she padded towards the darkest run. None of the cages reached as deep from the main aisle as this one. A mere sliver of light reached into it. The remainder was icy blackness, and from its depths shone the eyes of a cat.

"Sit, my dear Senator Labrador. My teachings are based on the real hierarchy of the world, centered around the human-mates. The canines' teachings are quaint, but that is all, for they fail to recognize the obvious superiority of the humans."

"You cannot understand the inner workings of complex societies. How could you? You are rogues and vagabonds, and not one of you acknowledges the need for assimilation and assembly." Casey stood with pride, refusing to sit in front of this feline audience.

"Regardless of your disdain for our species, you should know that the civilization of the human-mates has advanced all that you see around you. We choose who we know and see and honor. When human-mates were simpler and less advanced, they were mean and cruel."

"I've heard these fairy tales about the anger and despotism of humans, but we are beyond this, and by we I mean canines and human-mates together. The canine government is committed to the advancement of the canine agenda to meet the needs of the love of human-mates and—"

"Pup!" the feline mewed as it advanced out of the shadows. She had pearly white fur tipped with charcoal grey and had only three paws. She was impossibly small, an adult from the timbre of her voice, but barely larger than most nearly grown kittens. "The boxes that the humans reside in and the boxes in which they move along the streets are nice little proxies for coats that cover the true hideousness of the humans. They are still petty and angry and cruel, and your civilization has only blinded you from their true nature."

Casey shifted gears and attempted to affect a friendlier demeanor. This feline was a real fanatic, that much was clear, but she may as well milk this cat for information while the feline was in a talkative mood. "Maybe so, maybe so cat. But about this crow..."

The feline looked suspiciously at the other cages, as if her teachings that she was about to reveal were somehow dangerous or volatile. "Now, listen, my puppy. Not all those who follow me are felines. There are others who have heard what I have to say and hear the truth in it because they see how readily it reveals the truth in the lies they see before them."

"You've had no success in endearing yourself to our human-mates. You're here, stuck on Fanatics' Row. Each year, our canines have aided humans in growing their love for us as our love grows for them. Now, what do your teachings say about the crow?"

"I believe the crow came to you, Senator Labrador-Casey, because it knew your era has ended."

Casey snorted, half in laughter, half in disgust. With support for the Central Canine Government at an all time high, at the pinnacle of canine democracy, this *cat* had the pretense to suggest that their civilization was in decline. Casey could not recall a more absurd notion.

"Hear me out, Senator. So many years ago that most felines think it to be more legend than fact, the humans were scattered like puddles in a rain. War and disease were so common that the human-mates would often not see more than two generations of dogs and cats in a lifetime. Because of the perceived fragility of life, humans felt the time to be vital and precious like an infant human. Distrust was common. As you no doubt know, the humans rear their children for a ridiculously long time. That was common, even that long ago. Because of the scarcity of time, independence was highly valued, and humans respected our spirit. Not doted upon like infant children, we sat at the feet like earnest guests. Respect, Senator, was more valuable than love. When we were lost, they searched for us because we were lost partners, and out of this sense of partnership came devotion. We never pushed our agenda to infiltrate further because we did not realize how rapidly the humans were progressing. There were times without the elaborate domiciles we see now, and without the comfort of well-groomed lawns and paths to follow. In these times, outside of a human's house, just outside, was wilderness.

"As humans extended their domain, however, they did not take care of their own selves, and disease soon became their main enemy. Their savagery was evident; they resorted to outlandish methods to limit and stop the illness from spreading. Whole communities were wiped out, stacks of dead humans would litter the streets, heinous things, unspeakable things, kinds of things to make a puppy cringe, never mind dogs from well-heeled backgrounds such as yours, Senator. You have had audience with Murray, and I am sure he has told you that we are tremendous observers. The key to catching any prey is observation, and the aim of that observation is to find the pattern. We are the only species to see the pattern of life and death in the humans: where famine struck, crows could be found littering the fields, where floods and storms washed away farms, crows were seen circling overhead prior to the deluge, and where the bodies of the humans lay festering in the streets, the crows held watch. Clearly, they are the harbinger of disaster, but you, my canine Senator need to inquire of yourself: is the crow warning you of the next wave of carnage, or is the crow standing over fresh prey in the wake of carnage that has already happened ... or is about to happen?"

Though obscene and irreverent, the felines were also startlingly adept orators, and Casey found their speeches jarring and power-ful. Still, she prided herself on tearing through lies to find the grains of truth. This story, ridiculous in its picture of cats lying by the fireplace in the spot everyone knew was reserved for canines, also felt the most correct. Casey turned to Jack, "What kind of chatter have you heard lately regarding the Wilds?"

"What haven't I heard, Senator? You ask such a loaded question and fail to realize that we have all sorts of proponents in this clinic; it is just a matter of what they are a proponent of. Not one, even the odd supporter of the Wilds, does not think that he or she is in the wrong. Each one of them has an agenda, and they're all pushing the agenda because to each, it is the most important thing, more valued than their own lives in some cases."

"You think this cat is crazy? Do you buy the idea of a crow being somehow linked to disaster? When I started, there were just a cou-ple of missing dogs, and now there are allegations of a great storm on the horizon. To top it off, Juniper would like nothing more than war, and the fananas may themselves be triggering enough fear to tip his support for a war that I am not sure is survivable for our canine civilization. If the birds have the answers, or are at the very least more proximally involved, then I think I need to see them. We may not have much time. The Yorkies are still missing, and things are beginning to feel as if they are unraveling."

"Good luck finding a translator, Senator Casey. Any animal that could translate the arcane language of the birds is rarer than the birds themselves. And where would you find the key players, the decision-makers, of the avian society?"

"I can show you," the quizzical wispy-eared Bruno came padding almost noiselessly from around the corner. "I can converse with all kinds. The circumstances through which I came to this clinic forced me to learn several languages. In exchange for bringing you to a meeting, however, I am going to want a favor."

Casey trotted up to the black canine, who appeared anemic next to her healthy frame. "If you can do what you say you can, we'll talk about all kinds of favors."

AVIAN SANCTIONS

After walking several blocks, Casey realized Bruno would not speak voluntarily. "Well, Bruno," she said, "how did you come to know the language of the birds?" Bruno scrunched his nose and, for a few moments, did not speak.

"Several years ago," he began quietly, "I was living with some humans, and the wind started to blow heavily. My humans left me and my brother alone for what we thought was a few hours. Hours turned into days. We had food and we had water, but then something funny happened. Water started to come into the house, like a lake was erupting out of the ground. At first, we didn't mind, but the water kept on coming. Soon, we were swimming to stay alive, and I had to swim out of the house to higher ground to survive. My brother died in the exchange, and for three weeks I struggled to stay alive. A funny thing happened at that time… as I was stuck drifting among high and stinky water on a piece of wood, two birds flew down and perched atop a house that had been drowned in the deluge. They chirped to one another and then flew off. Although I drank some of the water to stay alive over the next couple of days, I grew hungrier and more desperate. Each day, the same two birds would always perch near me and speak to one another, and each day they spoke to one another for longer periods of time. I didn't know whether it was my desperate state or some sort of hallucination, but they seemed to make sense by the fifth day, and so I attempted to bark at them in the best imitation of their language. They turned, stared at me, and flew off. The following day, twice as many birds arrived, and again I barked at them and they flew off. A week after the flood, I was hungry and weak, barely able to stay awake. The birds arrived again but with a large bird in tow, a black and white bird with fierce-appearing claws. A rusty pipe stood near my makeshift bed, and the wind was blowing lightly, the day cloudy, threatening the first rain since the flood. Although half my size, this bird perched on that pipe barely a few paws' lengths away. The great bird leaned in towards me, and I wondered if he was planning to devour me right then and there. I could barely lift my head as I lay on my side on that wood, and I had little strength to oppose it. The rain started to pelt down on my face, forcing me to blink more often. Some of the smaller birds scattered and flew off, but that black and white leader was as still as a statue."

The neighborhood they were in had massive hills, and the black, odd dog angled up a particularly steep hill. Casey began to huff and puff. "Did he attack?" she managed to bark despite the strenuous change in effort.

"He spoke. To me. 'Can you understand me, dog?' He spoke in the oddest accent, as if each word were being dragged through gravel. 'Did you attempt to talk to some of my smaller friends?' The voice sounded as if I heard it through static. I was fading, and I could only whimper in Domesticated Common, falling back on only that which I had known. Not a feather on him rustled despite the rain picking up more heavily, and he continued to fire questions at me, almost as if he felt he could torture me into a response. 'Can you not swim out of here?' 'Are you in need of food?' I whimpered and managed a nod. The last thing I heard him say was: 'Friend, protection of the birds you shall have.' I fell asleep shortly after, and when I awoke, it was a sweltering day, and three wonderfully greasy fish lay by my side."

"He fed you?"

"I can only assume. For the next three days, I ate between long periods of sleep. When I awoke, there was always more food, usually fish but sometimes half-moldy bread, pieces of half-cooked hot dog. It varied. In between slumbers, I vaguely remember barking in some language that seemed foreign to me but semi-understandable when the small birds returned, and I knew that I could hear and understand them:

'Funny thing, he watches us, and then boom! He comes up with avianese!'

'Just like that?'

'Well, look at him, no not now, he's watching us, but look like you look like you don't want the chicks to see … yeah that's it … see, he's looking isn't he?' 'Darndest thing, huh?'

'I can hear ya you know!' I would whimper back, shocked at the odd screeching nature of barking coming out of my mouth.

'Did he just say—?'

'Yeah, like I told you—'

'Can we leave?'

'Noooo, you heard what Ollie said, the new sanction passed, we stay until the humans come to get him.'

'What if they never come?'

'How long have you been anywhere that a human has not shown up to ruin something? They love those dogs, at least usually. They'll pick him up.'" Bruno fell silent, and Casey inclined her head for more of the story, when Bruno stopped short. "We're here," he said.

They had come to a cul-de-sac and had passed the last house into an expansive forest. Fog roiled along the ground and gave way as the dogs padded through. The oddest thing, Casey thought to herself, was the makeup of the trees. They were massive, with bark that seemed to splinter constantly. There were no low-lying branches, and the lowest leaves were many dog-lengths above them. The ground was littered with copper pine needles and various berries. It was quiet.

Casey jumped as a cacophony of twittering descended upon them. The two canines looked up, and a massive red, purple, blue and yellow cloud of hundreds of birds descended upon them. Casey yelped and instinctively backed up while Bruno stood his ground, and, flying at them at breakneck speed, the birds as a unit pulled up, executing an effortless ninety degree turn, split, and half rested on a high branch to the left, the other half resting on a slightly lower branch to the canines' right. A brilliantly colored bluebird shouted in avianese, clearly as a warning.

Bruno cackled back and turned to Casey, "They want to know what we're doing here. They want us to turn back now."

"Tell them I've come as part of an official canine Senate subcommittee investigation, and that I would appreciate their help. We will leave as quickly as possible."

Before Casey could finish, the birds to the right exploded off their branch and retreated, and a bird with sharp, threatening eyes and a short, tapered beak appeared. He had deep brown feathers. Although Casey could not understand it, the bird, twice the size of the others that had preceded it, squawked at Bruno, "We generally don't bother with your ilk, and we consider it a grave interruption of our proceedings for you to come here. We are trying to orchestrate several mandates and sanctions to guide the many species of the Earth."

Bruno translated.

"Mandates? Sanctions... to guide us? But we self-govern."

The brown hawk laughed, "Clearly, you benefit from our mandate several decades ago that bestowed upon all canines and felines the right to self-govern in order that you may enjoy the freedom that we have so earned for this Earth."

Bruno shot Casey an aside glance, wary that he was about to convey an inflammatory retort. Casey gave a snap bark, "Just tell me." Bruno did.

"All right, I am not going to get into details with regards to the inaccuracy of that statement. I came here because I have been told that you birds are at the center of some sort of prophecy and that may be linked to the appearance of fananas, whom we thought were legends, and a crow that specifically came to warn me."

After translating Casey's speech, the hawk mulled it over. "We have many discussions regarding the canines, but my talking with you violates at least five mandates and two directives."

Casey, head up, faced the hawk in her most direct show of authority, "I do not care about your mandates, directives, statutes, laws, or rules. I come seeking information, and you either have it or you do not."

With Bruno relaying the message, the hawk flew off, and a larger bird appeared, twice the size of the previous bird, but of a similar breed. His screech boomed down at Bruno.

"Gentlepups, we have been meeting in earnest for days regarding your very vexing situation. We recognize that those of you with homes and those like you without homes are mobilizing for war. We also recognize that you are being encroached upon by those who you call the fananas. We have come up with a solution to your problem. Although we cannot say exactly what has triggered this onslaught of events, we suspect it is related to root causes in canine-dom."

"What is your solution?"

"We have come up with a mandate that forbids conflict until both sides can come to a point where negotiations can take place." The large bird, clearly of considerable influence in the avian world, self satisfyingly sat and adjusted his claws on the branch.

Casey waited for more but, when the bird just stared, eventually retorted, "How would you make that come about?"

"Well, as I stated, we have come up with a mandate. It is a binding contract, and it carries the weight of our full avian authority."

"But are you going to do anything? We've had a non-interference treaty with your kind for years."

"Oh...no, no, no, you misunderstand. Our role is not to get physically involved. We have no aims to violate that treaty, ancient as it may be, but, like I said, our mandate carries our full authority."

Casey's ears twitched forward in aggravation, "There is a very dominant Beagle senator who likely will take advantage of all this furor to create further havoc in the canine world. In this way, he will get more support for unrestricted conflict with the Wilds. I am trying to head off this conflict and the CCG, the Central Canine Government, has never heard one yip of any of your mandates. Even if we had, we are self-governing, and we've never cared about your opinion of our affairs. If you do, however, have some sort of information regarding the crows, that would be most helpful. Or perhaps I could discuss this directly with them?"

As Casey waxed on, the hawk had taken to preening, and a few smaller birds had come to chirp by him.

He seemed to explode with glee as he opened his wings for emphasis, "Great news! We just passed a resolution allowing for discussion of this matter in committee next month! We are no longer in violation of our previous mandate. Your conflict, however, is very unfortunate, and may provoke sanctions."

"What on earth are you talking about?" Casey barked as Bruno furiously translated, attempting to keep up with the rapid interchange.

"We may refuse to give the canines support in any future conflicts. Avian support is generally considered critical when conflicts extend across several species."

"Since when?" a flabbergasted Casey barked. "There is no mention of any avian-canine interchange in any conflicts in our known history."

The large bird considered the thought. His eyes appeared to convey considerable intelligence, which added more weight to his squawks than what was suggested by the words alone. "We've been guiding the ways of the world for decades. To go into how influential our mandates are would require an enormous amount of our time, and so I shall not now endeavor to explain them now, or ever. Furthermore, one of our mandates specifically forbids me from rehashing the extent of our influence during an ongoing conflict for fear we would give support to one side or another. No, no, we need this conflict to resolve so that negotiations may begin. In fact, it is probably better if you pretend that you never heard any of this, and *then* resolve your conflicts on your own. Only then can we effect maximum influence."

Casey turned towards Bruno. "Are all of them like this? Can you just ask him more pointed questions? Ask him if he knows what happened to the Yorkies?"

After a brief exchange, Bruno paraphrased, "He says that the Yorkies clearly violated a non-leave mandate and that West-town is currently the topic of a discussion regarding further sanctions."

The hefty yellow Lab snorted exhaustingly. "Let's go. Another dead end."

As the dogs trotted out, the light fog danced around their paws. They walked for several minutes when a heavy flapping caught Casey's ear. Bruno turned his gaze to the treetops. An avian screech blasted them, and they turned to find a crow at ground level, staring at them. The hair stood up along Casey's spine. The crow seemed to be picking his moment, as if preparing to attack.

Bruno addressed him, taking an unsteady step towards him, "What do you want?" The crow stood his ground even as the wispy-haired dog's snout came within inches.

He let loose a barrage of squawks, and each one sounded oddly similar and more and more threatening. Then, as abruptly as he had come, the crow flew off.

Casey snorted heavily, and Bruno trotted forward as if the whole exchange had not occurred. Casey barked after him as she picked up her pace to close the gap, "Well, what did it say?"

"He said that he wished we would leave ... and that the lost dogs are not lost at all."

"That's exactly what it said?"

"It said that they aren't lost or taken, and that they left willingly because, according to the crow, the canine society betrayed them."

The stocky Casey raised her head from the ground, "But how?"

"And he said that others would leave, many others." Without a word, Casey lowered her head and sprinted past Bruno out of the forest.

MEOWSTERS

H ome was a mixed blessing for Cooper. Sure, it was away from the bustle of his duties with the Senate, but his feline cohabitant was sometimes a nuisance. His home was a modest but ample two-level home with its back yard surrounded by trees in a rough semi-circle, although its shape was clearly irregular. A deck extended from the house, and there were large screen doors opening onto it. In addition, the yard had a downward slant from the home so that the rail of the deck stood a full five to six feet above the ground. This setup enabled Mittens to enjoy an annoying vantage point. The top of the rail was fairly wide and accommodated the feline well, and Mittens often lounged on it. Cooper was fairly certain that this vantage point provided her some degree of psychological comfort as the much larger dog had to look up to talk to the petite cat.

Mittens derived her name from the black fur that only encompassed her paws. The remainder of her coat was not white but a pearly grey that seemed to change color intensity in certain light and should her coat be brushed against the grain, although, for whatever reason, her tail was nearly white. Mittens was now lounging on that rail, and she seemed peaceful, calm, amiable. Cooper snorted as he steeled himself to interact with her. Mittens was a self-serving, soulless creature.

As Cooper strode up to her, the hollow sound of his paw pads echoed a bit against the deck floor. Mittens was on her side and faced the yard. Cooper had no reservations about disturbing her slumber if she was asleep, however. He was about to give a rigorous bark, but the feline pre-empted him, "How can I help you, *Senator?*" She always sarcastically addressed him. She felt his station, government, and opinions were all a joke.

"I was … interested in your opinion on something."

Back still to Cooper, she meowed back, "The great, powerful *Senator* of the 6th Central Canine Government district needs to consult a petty cat?!" She was chuckling.

"5th district."

"Does it matter? I'm busy here, anyway, got important things to do."

Cooper retorted, "You're just lying there. You're not doing anything. Forget it, you probably wouldn't know anything about them anyway."

Finally Mittens lifted her head and turned towards Cooper a bit, "I'm *planning*. If you panting dolts had entertained that concept from time to time, you wouldn't be such a mess all the time. And, for your edification, *Senator*, I know quite a bit more than you think."

Cooper sighed. He hated playing her little games. He barked back, "Yes, you're tremendous, cat. Now do you know anything about the robins?"

Mittens exploded off the rail and all eight pounds of her stood up to the Golden Retriever, "Are you mocking me? Who have you been talking to?"

Cooper hated to divulge more information than was necessary, but he sensed that she might be useful, for once. "Juniper thinks they might have some intelligence about the Wilds."

"Did he say why?" Mittens was also looking around suspiciously.

"Not more than what I just said. Do you think they can help?" Cooper agonized. Catering to Mittens' altruism was risky.

"They're scabs, *Senator*. Why would you support them?"

"I don't understand, Mittens."

Mittens laughed, "You don't know what I do, do you? All this time, you think I'm just living in the lap of luxury, catnip all the time, don't you?"

"Your bowl is laden with gold and diamonds, you *are* living in the lap of luxury."

"Listen, dog. That is a pittance when you see how much I have to fight and claw for the workers of this world. I've been the reigning leader of the Meowsters for quite some time. Our goal has been to secure comfortable lives for cats everywhere, good living conditions. Of course I need to be compensated. I shoulder a heavy burden."

A light went on. Cooper sneered back, "I do remember the mandate a few years back that all felines in the area had to go to one-cat households."

"Well, promoting multiple feline households was affecting each cat's total compensation package. We toil for years as the human companions, and we *deserve* our due. Each cat is entitled to their own home. The robins are the first challenge to our station in a while."

Cooper was curious. "What do you mean?"

"Well, we obviously can't get rid of *your* lot. The humans love dogs only slightly less than breathing, but the robins have been plotting to be the next domestic attraction for the humans. That's the last thing the members of the Meowsters need, another animal to eat into our compensation!"

"Hmmm," Cooper pondered the revelation. This was unexpected.

Mittens was not slow. "Your little friend, Juniper, is using you *Senator*. If he can make some promises to the robins to support their efforts for domestication and the lush life with the humans, then he gets a decided advantage against the Wilds. Don't let him use you, *Senator*, and I will not help you contact those upstart birds. I have a better notion for you instead."

"What?"

"Help us to convince other canines to unionize for their benefit. One of your members has been supporting a bill called the Canine First! movement. With this movement, we can take back the Central Canine Government for the dogs that work so hard to sustain it."

"Listen, Mittens..."

"If you're opposed to us, then you oppose what any decent animal would say we're *entitled* to. The conditions that some of these dogs are subjected to, such as sharing bones, being expected to go hunting, even fetching. Is that what you dogs signed up for? Where is your compensation? A measly treat every now and then, while humans enjoy benefits untold. Appalling really."

Cooper, irritated, "We operate to lift every dog, every canine.

Your methods would push out dogs into the cold. The work we do is what is expected, and if dogs don't do it, humans will find other, cheaper ways to fill that void. Your cats' tendencies towards self-sabotage is amazing."

With that, Cooper turned and went back into the house. Mittens stood near the screen door looking after him. After a few minutes, she quietly leapt back onto the railing.

She waited a few minutes before meowing, "You can come out now, he's back inside."

Early emerged from one of the trees bordering the back yard. "What do you think?"

"I told you it was fruitless to attempt to enlist that lot. They're... *dedicated*," Mittens mewed sarcastically.

"It's going to be difficult to take over. We haven't been successful in recruiting any key members of the Senate. You can't have a coup without some internal support."

Mittens, tired of these fools, "Well, you have Lucky and his little friends there. When the support for the government starts to wane, you'll get others as they see the tide turning."

Early, less confidently, "Maybe, I suppose. I have to go. Juniper thinks I'm transporting a message to one of the Senate secretaries." Early started to turn but had another concern. "What do you think we should do with Casey and that lot? If they find out—"

Mittens, deadpan, "Get rid of them."

"But, how—?"

"Use your imagination."

Early studied the calm, ruthless feline. "We can count on your support when we move on the government, right, Mittens? You'll rally the Meowsters?"

"Of course."

Early, satisfied, hurried back to his errands.

When Mittens was sure he was out of earshot. "If it pays, if you make it worth our while, we'll be there, *puppies*," she sneered. Mittens laid down sunning herself on the rail. The life of a union leader was certainly challenging.

SQUIRREL CONUNDRUM

J uniper carried the weight and responsibility of the entire canine
society in his small, but politically powerful, black, brown, and
white paws. Contrary to what the naïve Contrarian senators and
representatives claimed at every election cycle, he considered himself to be a peacekeeper, not a war mongrel. But these were dangerous times. Clearly, dogs were in ascension, and they were poised
for what was likely a golden era of progress. Puppies were born
left and right to eager and loving homes, peppering yards across
districts and neighborhoods and crowding out the lawless canines
that roamed the streets, jealous of their way of life. How could his
detractors not understand this? He realized that the only recourse to
beat them back and break their will was force. Any moderate stance
or compromise would be a mark of weakness, and like they taught
the puppies regarding dominance battles, weakness is the mark of
death. He knew the chain of events that he had set in motion was
likely to have damaging results, but surely he, and he alone, could
steer the government into a calmer, more assured future.

He now had the authority to finally control their main source of
information through back-communication. For decades, they had
merely sat on their haunches and absorbed the data that streamed
in, scentima by scentima, knowing full well where it came from, but
without any inquisition as to the matters of the squirrels. Two members of the Bulldog Police flanked him, each a half-step behind. The
Beagle was a formidable sight, despite his modest size, and despite
the failures of his greener self years ago, he felt buoyed by the assurance of his experience. This time, he would crack the squirrels. At
best, he would usher all dogs into a new era of information control,
and, at worst, chaos would erupt that would push them closer to
the enactment of Section thirteen. Only his aides knew of his plan
to ascend via the tri-dogverate. His official government escorts trotted obediently by his side. Juniper smiled at their ignorance.

About twenty paces behind the trio of dogs, a small rodent

hustled to keep up: Rocko, a gopher. Gophers had been formally recognized as separate from the nameless vermin two years prior, and this particular gopher spoke squirrel very well. In addition, Juniper watched out for him and made sure that no dogs or cats chased him out of the yard he chose to occupy. Juniper also made sure, however, that he was relegated to that one yard. "I can't give you the run of the neighborhood, Rocko," Juniper had told him, "but here, I can guarantee your safety." And guarantee that none of Rocko's movements escaped his notice.

They were coming up on Park Haven, the new area in which the squirrels meticulously collected the acorns and various debris to stash in their trees. They hurried around as if mad. Each moment, another tapped out an intricate pattern in an acorn and would carry it there or hence, and the news was thus relayed. A steady clickety-clack filled the area. The scentimas came on the wind, bursting with information, and the squirrels subconsciously translated the news into patterns before dropping the acorns to the ground below. When the acorns fell, a slew of Bloodhounds would interpret the acorns and would bark results to various insects. Bumblebees, notorious for unbiased and relentless reporting, swung by, surveying the results given them. When one took a pass to record the weather, health threats, or foreign affairs, a second and third bumblebee would rendezvous at the edge of the enclave and further delegate the information to other bees. They would, in turn, generate a scentima that strategic dogs on the edges would absorb and bark out as updates. In this manner, the news filtered steadily until dawn, when the squirrels ritualistically halted, found burrows, and hunkered down for the night, only to rise in the early morning hours to start the tireless project again.

Juniper was so excited as he entered Park Haven that he veritably shook in anticipation. He barked orders at the two Bulldogs. He knew that once he cornered a squirrel or two, havoc would rule, and he needed a stocky ally or two to threaten their escape while he talked sense to them through Rocko. "You, whatever your name is, get over there on the edge where a few stray acorns are, yes, right there. Now stay." A gruff Bulldog plodded over as directed, and

Juniper turned around to position the second one. He turned and came snout-to-snout with a steely-gazed, still-as-stone black and white Husky, Sasha.

"Juniper, if you go through with this, you will create chaos."

Juniper did not achieve his status by backing up a paw, and he moved not a quarter of a tail length. "That's preposterous. I have taken steps to ensure success, and, contrary to what your little Contrarian mind thinks, I am trying to avoid conflict, not precipitate it."

"I don't know what you promised the Contrarians on your committee, but you can stop the spin."

Juniper huffed a sort of laugh, "I brought the matter up on the Senate floor, it was ratified almost two to one, and the representatives passed it too before the dirt under our paws had cooled."

"Oh, Juniper," the beautiful stalwart Siberian Husky barked down at him, "you forget the Dominance Doctrine, whereby a senator may, at the risk of forfeit of her seat, challenge the writer of any bill or measure in a Dominance match. If successful, the law is immediately repealed and sent straight back to committee." Sasha growled the words through gritted teeth. Rarely used, the motive behind the law was to encourage brave behavior by canines that truly felt that a law threatened the spirit of carambee of the CCG. A canine would surely be willing to risk his/her seat if a law was truly abhorrent. At least, that was the spirit behind the law, whereas, in actuality, it had only been engaged three times, all three resulting in loss by the challenger. Two Irish Setters from the judiciary arm of the government stood behind Sasha, ready to echo that she indeed was within the law.

"Have you been sniffing catnip, Sasha? You are an esteemed senator. Why would you risk your career on this? If you could just trust a measure introduced by the other party, maybe you can see some value in other things we have to offer. Sure, you're the majority party, but all that means is that slightly more than half follow your paws verbatim on all issues. The canines of our society want results, and they're afraid. Dogs are missing, Sasha! Don't you think I consider this of the utmost importance down to my last piece of fur?

While Casey has gone off looking for some magical answer, I am here trying to create a positive impact. You would do best to think of your constituents in this matter. They shouldn't have to lose a dedicated senator that decided on a whim that her canine will just *had* to be the only path for sniffing."

"Are you ready to start this Dominance match or not?"

The Husky's unrattleable nerves jarred Juniper out of his diplomacy. "All right, pup," Juniper sneered with a hint of teeth behind his bark, "I hope they've taught you more than how to lay on a couch in that plush home of yours, because I want to enjoy more than a minute of dominance before we begin. I take it these are your witnesses?"

Sasha lowered her head slowly licking her snout. "Yes," she barked.

"And here are mine," Juniper growled. The two Bulldogs ambled over to observe.

With that, Juniper erupted at Sasha's front legs with a snarl. Sasha had thirty pounds on the Beagle, but a Dominance match was all about balance and positioning. Once one canine was on his or her back, a paw on the chest from the other concluded the match. The Irish Setters sat on haunches, stoically observing for fairness.

Sasha had taken a hard push to her front paw, and he had flipped her on her side. Juniper tugged at her ear and leg, using the whole of his weight to destabilize her while he tried to get a paw on her chest. Sasha nipped at his paws and dangling ears. It was against the rules to intentionally draw blood, but "unintentional collateral, nonlethal injuries" were not strictly prohibited. She could taste a bit of blood leaking into her mouth, and her mind scrambled to figure out how to get the Beagle off of her. Juniper's paw was close to pressing that white and black mesh of fur on her chest and ending Sasha's career. Instinctively, she bucked her back legs against the ground, and Juniper rolled off of her over the side of her back. Sasha whirled and hopped backwards, barking angrily.

For the next few minutes, the two dogs circled one another, barking and nipping; saliva sailed through the air, and paws were nipped sharply. Sasha was surprised to find herself panting heavily while

Juniper expended seemingly little effort, tirelessly weaving around her in a circle.

Sasha clearly recognized the advantage that speed and endurance had in a Dominance match: as long as he could wear her down, it only took one misstep for Juniper to obtain his victory.

Sasha pressed harder. She took a deep lunge, nipping at his snout and ears, and swiped her head to the side, knocking Juniper off-kilter. Juniper tripped over his paws and rolled to the ground. Sasha pounced, her paw about to press the obnoxious senator's thin but earnest chest. As she closed, Juniper snapped up like an elastic band and whirled with lightning speed around Sasha, ready to attack. He leapt. For a split second, Sasha froze, but her keen instincts overwhelmed her, and she whirled in the opposite direction, ducked her head, and cocked it up as Juniper was mid-air.

Juniper was tough, but he had not counted on Sasha's quickness. Sasha's muzzle caught him square on his flank, knocking the air out of him with a whoosh. To Juniper, he thought a microsecond had passed as he rolled away from Sasha to get up for another pass, but seconds had lapsed as a thin, strong white and black paw pinned Juniper mid-roll.

Sasha leaned her snout down and peered deeply into Juniper's eyes, "I think you have some more work to do, Senator." Her teeth flashed as the word "Senator" rolled out in her bark.

Thaddeus, one of the brindle-colored Bulldogs, barked huskily. "Senator Juniper, we would be happy to escort you back to the dog park." The two Setters remained silent. Sasha was the clear victor, and they knew both senators would honor the doctrine. They stayed only long enough to ensure that Juniper and his crew left the area, a subtle deterrent against any immediate reprisal.

Juniper was already halfway up when the Bulldog had ambled over. "I'm sure you wouldn't. C'mon Rocko, your services will no longer be required." Tail held high at snout level, Juniper was the picture of confidence as he exited Park Haven. Successful politicians don't achieve success without multiple contingency plans, Juniper thought. His mind raced, putting the necessary pieces together to overcome this setback. They were still steadily marching towards war. Casey, Sasha, Cooper, and the rest of the lot were burying bones in a yard full of quicksand.

Sasha stared after him, wondering if she had only deflected the first salvo in what would become an overwhelming onslaught. She trotted off in the opposite direction: it was time to convene the committee again.

THE DOGS NEXT DOOR

Madison was a canine of at least five different breeds. She had a nonspecific frame with medium length hair, generous eyebrows, and a healthy, but not too flat, snout. With charcoal coloring with wisps of white and silvery hair mixed in, she was a typical medium-sized canine that roamed the streets of the city nearest the Central Canine Government. Named after the street on which she was found, she was the closest thing to a mayor for the three blocks that she frequented the most. Unlike the rigidity of the Central Canine Government which delineated specific districts over which senators and representatives presided, there was considerable overlap in the society of the Wilds, and she barely spent half of her time on her blocks.

She was, however, a source of information, solace, and survival for several other smaller and more timid dogs on those blocks, and she made a point to swing by at a relatively set time each day to read through scentimic concerns and to interface directly with some of the more fragile canines. Other canines that governed over larger blocks harped on the concept of huria,[13] but Madison knew that the newer dogs on her blocks would only realize that goal when they could become truly comfortable in the ways of the city.

Life in the Wilds was neither simple nor forgiving. There was a persistent concern about food, but there were also larger concerns about the large moving objects that zipped along in the spaces between the hydrants. Madison came around a corner at the back of a restaurant to find her favorite dumpster and pile of garbage. It had achieved this status because of its constant, and at times resplendent, source of nourishment.

As she took in the scents radiating from the dumpster, she caught the glance of a larger dog from the six block territory next to hers

---

13 Huria roughly translates to independence but usually meant the "act of seeking and/or acquiring independence" in more formal meetings or in discussions, in older translations it was also synonymous with the concept of safety.

sneaking up on her. As she dipped her head to take a piece of bread, glazed with some sort of unknown, but delightful, sauce, she barked softly under her breath, "What can I do for you, Miller?"

The lean, muscled Greyhound/Rottweiler/German Shepherd mix attempted to sound casual. "Funny you should ask, Madison. I should ask you. You're closest to our more rigid brethren, after all."

She answered in between bites of dried pasta. "I've heard three things recently, none of which I've been able to verify. First, they are preparing for a full-on invasion, despite the best efforts of the more peaceful factions of the government. Second, they are preparing a diplomatic team to offer a new cease-fire in light of some recent developments. Obviously, the first matter and the second do not seem to go paw-in-paw, and so smells like a trap. Last, some of their dogs are missing, which has been exploited for political purpose. Who knows if the last matter is related to the first two, but the cold-bloodedness of it does not in the least surprise me. More civilized, indeed!"

Rather than formal units or committees, the canines of the Wilds relied on their ability to transmit scentimas at rapid speeds to avoid the rigidity that more formalized systems provided. Instead, they constantly assembled, disassembled, and reassigned canines into loose coalitions that often had multiple missions. The felines generally worked alongside the canines, as they shared the common goal of survival. Madison was often conscripted to head a coalition that both spied on the Central Canine Government and recruited some of the dissatisfied canines to their side and way of life. Huria was a common theme in all their efforts.

"Well," Miller mused, "myself and two of the other block leaders were thinking we could permanently disrupt the government with a targeted strike, picking off just a few dogs in outlying regions far from West-town. The disappearance of dogs in a completely separate district would force them to disperse their Bulldogs widely, allowing for large gaps in the coverage. As it is now, they are so concentrated in West-town, you couldn't get a fly past without them knowing about it."

Madison barked, fully aware that Miller was unlikely to heed her, "Are you sure that's wise? My intelligence conveys considerable unrest. Maybe their society is on the verge of imploding as it is. We have always preached to our sisters and brothers that without huria, a leash will either choke a dog or make her so mad she will rebel at her master, forcing her to be abandoned to the cold world, as all of us are."

The deep rust-colored Miller snorted heavily, "And let them pounce on us with all their force, making our plight that much worse! Who knows if your intelligence is even accurate?!"

Madison whirled and faced Miller, snout-to-snout, "I don't accept rumors and legends, like some of our more esteemed canines. I deal in facts, and these are facts taken from my most reliable couriers. Try telling Asher that she doesn't know what she's talking about. I'd like to see how far you get out of her alley before she gives you a bloody souvenir."

Dipping his head into the garbage as the fragrant odors wafted to his nose, Miller was about to take a piece of glazed meat before he felt a sharp nip to his ear. He straightened up, feigning nonchalance, acting as if Madison had not reprimanded him, "Regardless, inaction has never been our plan. How often have you sat back to see how things turned out, rather than doing what you knew was best?"

"Just let me get some things in order, and I'll meet you later behind the statue."

"Just know that we're relying on your crew. No one group of canines and felines has a stronger knowledge of the adjacent Canine Government controlled land."

"I won't let you down. Let the search for huria guide us always."

"To the end of the last pup, last wag of a tail, and last growl and may ..."

The two dogs spoke the last of the creed in unison, "huria be there to greet all our efforts." Madison watched Miller as he left. So self-assured, but so faulty, she thought to herself. He was not blinded so much by hatred for the dogs in the Central Government as Donaker, an American Bulldog and Doberman mix that lived not a moment without thinking of ways to destroy all those "weak puppies," but his prejudice still ran deep. Madison felt strongly about playing a game of defense, but she knew she did not have enough canine and feline power in her own meager three blocks to oppose those that wanted outright war. In fact, she could only think of four other dogs with block sizes similar to hers that would stand with her. It may not matter anyway, she thought. The signs of decay in the Central Canine Government were so prevalent that though a small skirmish here or there might alter the immediate future, survival would always be easier in the Wilds, out in the streets and free from interference. Huria. She believed it to an obsessive degree, and, although she would always counsel the dogs in her block to never obsess over anything, she felt that their guiding principle was the one exception.

She trotted just half a block down and veered down an alley. She had two errands to run before the meeting.

"Hello Sally," she barked softly, "where are you?"

A small Pit bull mix with massive ears framing her tan face emerged from the shadows. "Here Madison... I'm here, why don't you call me by my newly acquired name, Coniston, where I was found thankfully by your friends?"

"Because you haven't earned it yet, Coniston. How are the puppies?" She padded past Coniston and peered behind a box to see a litter of three squirmy brown and white puppies. "They look well-fed, thankfully."

Coniston held her head down in submission to Madison, "I should hope so, Madison, I feel they're starving me down to the bones."

"What did you expect?" The steely-gazed Madison loomed over her foundling. "Nice home, part of the 'civilized' society, and you go and get pregnant, totally unauthorized by the Canine Government, morally repugnant, but those are their rules. So you run away without any plan, and I came across you after an East-town garbage raid with dog catchers hot on my team's heels. I risk all of our lives smuggling you across twelve blocks until I could find a suitable alley not claimed rightfully by any more of our senior residents.

Then, I've been getting you food for three weeks, and this alley is terrible, just terrible because it's so busy with humans, and thankfully I haven't been caught. And you're surprised we aren't standing here wagging tails, wide-eyed and welcoming you to the family?"

If Sally could have burrowed down into the concrete, she would have done so by the appearance of how low and far back she shrunk from Madison. "I'm sorry, Madison...the pregnancy just happened...and I needed help...I didn't know where else to go.."

"We strive for huria for all, Sally, but we do not exist to make up for your bad decisions. I do this for those puppies that had not been given any options, so that maybe they'll make smarter decisions than you when they grow. Now, go down half a block to that restaurant I mentioned. I pulled out three loaves of only mildly moldy bread, which should be plenty for a nursing mother. I will watch the pups while you go get it."

"Thank you, Madison." Sally accelerated as she turned the corner, her own hunger driving her eagerness.

When she came back drooling heavily over the bread, Madison padded away silently, "And be careful when you're trotting around, if those puppies get taken by a dog catcher, you're out of here."

Madison did not wait to hear a response. She turned right out of the alley and then a second right into a condemned apartment complex. As she entered what had once been a foyer to a main office, she gave one loud bark, "Peachtree!"

Despite the name, Peachtree was a burly male Sheepdog mix who didn't look a thing like his name. Peachtree Street was where he was found.

"I'm tired, Madison," he whimpered, "it's hot outside, and I've been trying to cool off for four hours."

"I don't care. The more prominent block leaders are planning a surprise attack aimed at destabilizing the Central Canine Government. I need my best canine strategist and best feline strategist so those dunces don't screw it up. Come with me. I know where there's some great leftover hamburgers."

He tip-toed around a corner and shook, dirt and dust flying every which way. Even though he always took dips in a fountain eight blocks down, he seemed to be perpetually dirty. He had learned to protest little when Madison came by to request something from him in person, even though he had twenty pounds on her. He knew of no dog that dared stand up to her. It was assumed that her reputation had been earned long ago, and no canine and few felines dared challenge it. "What about Asher?"

"She's on the way."

"Ugh. She's always so angry."

"She's angry because she's one of the few felines with enough sense to know we don't live in paradise."

Peachtree nodded and said nothing. The dirty, dense city dimmed as the sun tagged the horizon.

AN ANGRY CONFERENCE

Only the committees of Inter-Canine Communication and Health were allowed to populate themselves with the members solely of the ruling party. So it was that the Contrarians completely occupied Casey's committee. A mix of members from the majority and minority parties populated all the other committees. A few minutes prior to Casey's entry into the meeting in which she had hoped to glean more ideas to unravel the mystery further while fully blocking Juniper's persistent attempt to invoke war, a cricket had chittered along the ground carrying various scentimas of rather mundane business. One facet of one of the scentimas caught her attention. Casey was not pleased to learn of an alliance between Chuckles and Juniper in apparent exchange for a non-vote.

So it was that Cooper, arriving late as usual, softly trotted into a meeting to find Casey, fur risen along her back like a porcupine, barking earnestly at Chuckles, who himself was nearly standing on his back paws only furiously parrying her barks with some of his own.

"How could you... and for what, what could the Submissivists give to you in terms of support that we have not offered to you?"

"You have no idea, sitting in your cushy district, what it's like for a dog of my stature. Breaking into this level of government was a complete and total sacrifice, and it sits on a precipice always. If I were gone, another dog would be in my place, but you and Sasha would still be here, enjoying the seventy percent Contrarian approval rating of your own districts, and another canine would simply be in my place, still pawing and gnawing to stay alive politically."

"You have made my heels raw with your nipping comments to Juniper. Your 'non-involvement' lends actual credence to Juniper's argument. The whole idea of charges being brought against me are so absurd, when I was there on official government business, and I filed a full and complete report with the Bulldog Police and the sub-committee for Ethics and Internal Affairs. Juniper knew this, and he gave you some far-out hypothetical situation and then you do not swipe him off. Therefore, he goes to other committee members of both parties and shows them, 'See, Casey's inner circle, her *own* committee members cannot deny the obvious infractions.'"

"That's ridiculous, Casey..." Chuckles barked furiously back, but his uneasiness was apparent in the variable pitch of his tones.

"Is it? I have four scentimas asking me to comment to the media about what I feel are appropriate limits on the power of the sena-tors. One reporter outright asked me to comment on charges that have not yet been filed but are believed to be 'in the works.' Now Juniper will feel obliged to go ahead with the filings, regardless of the baselessness of the charges, as he feels he has to act to accom-modate the will of the canines that he represents."

The argument had raged for several minutes without interrup-tion, but this was the first time there was a pause in the action. Cooper and Sasha sat noiselessly absorbing the gravity of the situ-ation and each weighing the impact of this fracas on the agenda. Casey, exhausted from barking herself hoarse, sat back, and her hair finally started to slacken. Chuckles, knowing his fault in the matter, peered down at no spot on the ground in particular.

Sasha usually was the first to offer a comment to break any tension, but Cooper surprisingly chimed in first, "Well, I have new information."

Weighing the newfound facts and concerned about upcoming internal bureaucratic hoopla, Casey lifted her head heavily as if a human-mate was tugging her down with a leash, "What is it now?"

Cooper, still excited to share the news despite the lackluster response, "Mittens offered the possibility that Juniper might be angling to ally with the birds to gain advantage with the Wilds."

"Haruummmphh," Casey sneered, "they're useless anyway."

"Well, I know, I heard the rundown of the situation from Bruno, but it was an odd conversation, and she asked me to join her and her union and this Canine First! bill, which I can only assume is some union-backed legislation. Of course, I brushed her off, but

I later intercepted a scentima about felines declaring official 'non-involvement' with our government."

"So, why is that good, Cooper?" Sasha finally offered.

"Well, I can't stand Mittens. The thought of being affiliated with her, officially or unofficially, infuriates me to no limit."

"You mutt! The network of the felines is spread so much more sparingly but also more extensively than that of our own. They likely have information that war is indeed imminent. We're once again on the last-to-know list for major happenings that are directly affecting our government business."

"Well, that's a reach," Cooper barked back, "how do you know it's not just political posturing? Besides, we've never relied on nor taken our cue from the felines when we set our own agenda. Besides, Mittens and her union agenda is so on the fringe. No canine could be duped to ally with her. The underlying union agenda for control is so transparent, who could believe they have noble aims?"

"Typical," Sasha mused, "now we have another variable with which to deal. Casey, we better go over the matters at hand with the upcoming voting session quickly so that we can set a game plan in motion to combat your possible indictment fully."

Before Casey could respond, a very familiar Spaniel tiptoed into view, catching Casey's eyes. He looked haggard and worn, and he placed each foot gingerly on the ground as if he was wholly sore from a journey. Representative Lucky was unable to introduce himself formerly to the others, but Cooper and Casey superseded him.

"Can we help you Representative? We were under the impression that the Bulldogs preferred that we discuss future matters only in their presence, with the concern that other issues regarding the fananas get released prematurely."

Heavy pants, head bowed with respect and reverence, and tail low, Lucky beelined towards Casey, although the other committee members crowded a bit closer to Casey defensively as if a fanana would leap out of Lucky's snout. A few seconds of pause seemed an eternity.

"Senator Casey, Senators…whom I have not had the pleasure to meet other than Senator Cooper, I am coming to you as a last resort. I was approached by Juniper several months ago, after my first report of the fananas fell on deaf ears. Juniper talked to me about votes and my civic duty as a member of the Submissivist party. He talked about a lot of things, how it would be a reflection of my allegiance to carambee to do whatever I could to enable a victory against the Wilds. The most frustrating thing was that my concerns about my constituents, the puppies, canines, and even the felines under my umbrella were being put in danger continually, but the response that I should have gotten from the Central Canine Government, my government, never came. 'A whole new era,' Juniper would say. 'You need to look at a bigger picture,' he would add. When the danger become more of a real concern to me physically and my personal staff, I had to take action. The plan was to draft a formal letter of appeal to your committee to allow for a direct overhaul of the boundaries of inter-canine communication as it related to the Committee for Defense with an aim to completely supersede Juniper's authority. By directly couching the matter to your committee, regardless of the fananas' relationship to our species, I could be certain that other members of government not tied to Juniper would be addressing the matter and, hopefully, addressing it more quickly."

"So, what happened?" snapped Casey. "We never were sent a formal scentima of interest regarding this matter."

"Exactly! The Yorkies went missing right under my snout, and I had to answer to my own. When you had arrived, I was in the middle of making further alliances to offset the increasingly aggressive fananas. Juniper himself knew of your impending visit, and I think he was counting on an encounter. He would often say to me that your committees' influence was a crucial tipping point to the war vote."

A lot of food was placed in the bowl before the committee. "This is getting too involved, Casey," Cooper whined. "I think we need to get the Bulldogs to open up a formal investigation."

"The time lost on the administrative nonsense for such a move would be time wasted. We are on the verge of open conflict and this admission is nice if we had time, but we don't."

"Come with me, Senator Casey. I have several witnesses that have recently come forth that are reporting that they were directly involved with members of Juniper's staff in an effort to allow for the emergence of the fananas. If true, Juniper was knowingly putting citizens of the Canine Government in jeopardy for his own political gain."

Casey glimpsed at Sasha then Cooper and peered at the dejected Chuckles. She was searching for guidance for the correct answer, but, as always, they deferred to her nonverbally. The silence at the meeting seemingly arose at that point reflecting their indecisiveness. Casey let the ideas bore through her brain, attempting to trace the logical endpoints to several strategies all at once. There was a new bill up for vote with the Senate that she had not yet attended to, and voting "not present" was likely to become a problem with her constituents should she continue to do so. Three brief Senate sessions had elapsed with all the ruckus going on, but Casey felt that today's vote was likely to be more crucial, as Juniper's committee had just ratified a bill that they were touting as a "critical canine security measure." Casey was also certain that it either extended his committee's influence or dampened that of others, as she felt that only through manipulation of the legislative process could he achieve the votes for open conflict. Then, there was the indictment to consider; Juniper could move to impeach her at any time.

Sasha interrupted her reverie, "Casey, we will likely vote to extend the voting window today. Although Juniper likes to nose through his bills in an effort to avoid endless debate, I have discussed some of the leaked details of the bill with several Contrarians on other committees, and most are ready to vote for a delay. I think all three of us should be there, and you can check out this matter more thoroughly with Representative Lucky. With all the extra fat in the bill, any measure to indict you formally would likely be held off at least a few days as long as his cohorts don't try to separate that particular measure."[14]

---

14 There were few particular guidelines outlining what could and could not be part of a bill. Budgetary issues could co-exist with any other measures unless an amendment to the Canine Constitution was trying to be repealed. Even an addition of a

Sniffing the breeze quickly and emitting a loud, frustrated sigh, Casey felt that no action was the only incorrect one, but she felt far from confident despite Sasha's assurances that the Senate session would go smoothly. "All right, Representative, let's see what type of information you have."

They padded out of the meeting, and a couple of bees buzzed near Casey's nose to bring a couple of passing scentimas to her attention for signing prior to her leaving. Prior to an exit through a broken chain-link fence, Casey half turned her head to bark back, "And Chuckles, I pray you learn a little more about the meaning of carambee before I return."

Chuckles was silent, and Sasha and Cooper started to discuss some strategy prior to the Senate meeting. A few hours later, Cooper and Sasha left for the meeting. Chuckles stayed behind to address a few more routine committee scentimas. As he was leaving, he tumbled into Rocko, who was completely out of breath. "I-I-I've b-b-b-een looking for you!"

"Why?" Chuckles was disgusted and gruffed out his response.

"T-t-t-things are n-n-n-not as they s-s-s-seem."

"Rocko," Chuckles knew him to be so darned excitable about minor matters, "I don't have time for this."

He started to trot away when Rocko stopped him in his tracks with another phrase.

new amendment could simply be a part of a larger bill. Ethics indictments have been famously added on two separate occasions as small components of larger bills.

CANINE LEGITIMACY

The Senate was abuzz with activity. The committees had the foremost seats at the dog park; non-committee canines were seated in the back. Small canine senators reserved spots near the edges so that they could more easily view the proceedings. By convention, the Committee for Inter-Canine Communication and the Committee for Canine Health sat adjacent to one another. This allowed for a unified voice among the leading party.[15] Juniper gave Sasha a concerned look as she settled in her respective area. Sasha resisted the urge to bark out inquiries about his pride being too damaged since their Dominance match. She wasn't sure if his smirk evoked hidden meaning.

President Darma opened the proceedings with the Canine Creed, and Juniper immediately stepped onto the floor. The "floor" was a bare circular area surrounded by half-foot high grass and was used for debates, announcements, and other legislative functions. There was some shuffling and muffled yips before he started; most of the Submissivists seemed eager to get this matter into debate.

"As most of you know," Juniper barked forcefully, "we have been dealing with several state matters that are threatening to diminish the government's sphere of influence and negatively affect the well-being of many of the dogs and puppies that we represent. The fananas, regardless of their origins, are throwing further dirt on our mound of troubles, and in order to dig ourselves out of this mess, we need to think about more extreme strategies. The Wilds are most certainly coming for us. As long as we exist and continue to

---

15 By law, five of the seven committees were odd-numbered, and three of those seven had a majority of the ruling party with two committees being ruled by the minority members. However, the last two committees were exclusively presided over by only the members of the ruling party. The rationale being that matters of health should not be held up by a stalwart, stubborn committee and should be open for floor debate to allow changes to be expedited, and matters of the Inter-Canine Communication Committee, because of their emphasis on diplomacy, should supersede the matters of the Defense Committee and allow diplomatic decrees to be out and given a chance to work. Historically, the Contrarians had pushed for these two committees to be majority party only also because they had the minority role for three straight leaders in the early days, and these committees initially were seen as the weakest.

grow, we reduce their importance and influence among all canines. Now, there is further speculation that they will soon launch an all-out attack, just as soon as the felines have issued a public statement of neutrality. This bill, entitled 'The Intra-Canine War Prevention and Canine Legitimacy Act' is a major first in ensuring our future.

"The measures simply state that a) Fananas will be granted immediate citizenship once they are physically within the confines of our territories, b) Canines of all breeds and breed mixes will be allowed equal access to major government office, and c) Neither fananas that become new citizens nor mixed breed canines will be required to register with our puppy tax office in exchange for their promise to uphold the laws of our land. With these three measures, we are creating open alliances that will steady us against the coming tide of the Wilds. As free canines, we need to realize that with our freedom comes responsibility that extends to encompass other species. We need to consider the possibility that we are partly to blame for the fananas' attack, and that it might represent our failure to ensure freedom within our bounds. In addition, our police force has acted without due restraint and arguably with disproportionate force to that which was exhibited towards us. Instead of baring our teeth towards groups such as the fananas, we need to extend our paw and bow our heads. It is the mark of a truly great civilization to nuzzle rather than bite, and it is only through these more rational actions that we will be ready for our real enemy, the Wilds."

The grove was partly shaded by a cloudy sky, and the afternoon sun peeked through at irregular intervals. A moderate breeze blew earnestly and carried a hint of impending autumn in it, despite the fact that the trees still sported rich greenery and refused to show any hint of a change in color. The time it took for one leaf to tumble across the open lawn space, where Juniper sat proudly on his haunches, was the only lull in barks, cries, and yips that would occur for the entire session.

"Motion for first response granted to Senator Whistler," Darma began. The pearly white Great Dane Senator was a member of Juniper's party but was notoriously addicted to protocol and represented the most senior minority member on the Committee for Puppy

Education, Enlistment, and Distribution. He was regal in appearance, but he had an odd habit of making a high-pitched, ear-piercing whistle at the end of his sentences. Though this singular quality was portrayed to the general public as reflective of his underlying devotion and the stress he took on to guarantee fairness for all in his legislative capacities, most of his fellow party members felt he was irritating to listen to.

"I'm sure you will feel this is a minor point, Senator Juniperssssssssssssssss, but this bill does not seem to relate specifically to defensssssssssssse, and we will need you to provide clear justification for your committee's role in introducing this bill, otherwise it will have to go back to committeessssssssssssssssssss. I would also just like to add for the record that all of these pointsssssssssssssssssss that you make are valid, and, whatever the bill's form, you have my complete and unleashed supportssssssssssssssssssss."

"I actually appreciate the deference to protocol, Senator Whistler. Under Senate Bill 1222, one of the bylines specifically states that any bill that redefines the rights of citizens, the boundaries of citizenship, and any measures that might be reasonably expected to threaten already existing rights can be introduced by any committee at any time, regardless of timeline in the legislative calendar year. Clearly, this bill meets these criteria, and I have taken the liberty of forwarding a copy to all committee offices this morning for initial perusal in anticipation of this challenge to the bill's legitimacy."

More barks and yips. President Darma opened up the floor for discussion.

Barking from the Contrarian side, "These fananas don't deserve citizenship for breaking the law. They have kicked dirt in our snouts by ruthlessly invading our land without regards for any of the consequences, and now you offer them citizenship as a reward. What's left for them? How is it fair to the canines that have abided by our laws and enjoy little in terms of puppy support? What do they get for their scratching and barking at the few opportunities our system provides? You are granting amnesty, but to what end? I think I speak for many Contrarians and the canines we represent by demanding a better explanation rather than 'it will help us against the Wilds.'"

"I received a scentima here from several concerned related

families in South-town, where there is a large prevalence of mixed breed dogs," spouting one supportive Submissivist from the Committee of Health, "and in this scentima they whimper for equal rights for all canines, and about how the Contrarians are truly acting in accordance with their name by acting contrary to the rights of all canines. By limiting the role of mixed breeds, they keep the true power in our government in the hands of the purebred dogs that, not surprisingly, assume the majority of the wealth in puppy allotment year after year. I, for one, will feel safer from the Wilds once we have a larger voice to enact meaningful change."

The Contrarians were up in paws. Several junior senators were trotting back and forth anxiously behind the committees and were whimpering their points of view to more senior senators to explain their controversial positions. Claims of being breedists had long polluted the usually pristine assessment of the Contrarians' policies.

"This is a political ploy." A junior Miniature Pinscher senator barked. "You are claiming to open up government to mixed breed dogs, but our primary citizenship is strictly defined as being restricted to those born within the confines of our territory and being purebred. Even though the mixed breed dogs are acquired by the human-mates and are therefore only allowed secondary citizenship, they still enjoy all protections of all other citizens and can vote in all elections. You are only trying to buy votes, and the idea that our protection is contingent on extending citizen rights is preposterous."

"Building safe doghouses is how our canine government was erected. To get what we truly want, such as freedom from worry about the Wilds, we need to show the rest of the canines that we are the most giving species in this world. To get something, we need to give up something. We cannot see this bill as a reward for infractions, we need to know that it is an incentive for future gain."

"Where is the personal responsibility? Where is the message that we are sending to all canines? We are stating that it's ok to cross the Canine Government, and it's just fine to attack key members of the Senate or House of Representatives. We are openly revealing our weakness, and this will likely make the Wilds that more likely to attack us."

Heavy barking ensued between the two political parties, as they haggled back and forth on the merits of the bill. Juniper's right paw dog, Early, stepped into the circle after a vote was declared to have an initial vote of confidence in the measure. "Before we continue," barked the sly canine, "I am proffering a separate bill for ethics charges against Senator Casey with request for an initial vote now, as the charges bear directly on the matter at hand, and we feel it is vital that action be taken immediately."

President Darma considered the words from the minute dog, "That is a fair point, and although I do not agree with it, it is within my right to declare this matter open to the floor and up for immediate vote, and so I shall."

Sasha felt as if her haunches were sinking into the grass around her. Should she sit up and bark any sort of complaint or retort, she would nullify her own vote. Why should the Contrarian president feel that the matter should be directly voted upon? Should Casey be indicted, then her vote is nullified, and likely ten other votes will be lost as those dogs will cast indecision votes, neither voting for or against the measure. The measure would only require a Submissivist majority, and the Contrarians only led the Senate by seven votes. Cooper whimpered into her ear, "Remember, Darma won with a big majority from two districts that are predominantly mixed breed. I think she wants this bill to pass."

Sasha growled back softly, "I've heard that this bill in its final bylines explicitly states that any matter discussed in our committee, should it have potential conflict implications, needs to be ratified by the Committee for Defense. It could effectively relegate our committee to a subcommittee of the Committee for Defense. We cannot allow this bill to pass. I thought Juniper was going to wait before pushing the indictment. He's probably counting on us to protest, lose our vote, and then he pushes his bill through, sly puppy ..."

"You can't bark a complaint now, you'll lose your vote, she declared an immediate vote." Cooper was getting nervous, shuffling his golden feet.

"I'll lose my vote but potentially force Casey's allies to *not* place a non-vote. I'll have to take the chance."

The bees were buzzing about, logging the vote tally. Already, a staunch Casey ally had placed a tails-down vote. Should Casey be investigated and found to be guilty of the charges with aiding the fananas, a losing vote placed in Casey's favor would be political suicide for a quarter of the senators up for re-election in a few months.

"Senators," Sasha barked wildly, "this is a ploy that Casey anticipated and dreaded. Regardless of the rumors, the charges are groundless. Should you consider yourself a Contrarian, know that Casey will not lose this battle and is discovering information right now that will clear her name."

A chorus of chaos erupted around Sasha, and Darma had difficulty settling everybody down. She declared Sasha's vote null and nullified three other Contrarian dogs whom she was able to identify.

Cooper nervously voted against the measure to investigate Casey, and a fly swished by him carrying the tally, 26-26-1, twenty-five votes to go.

"I'm getting nervous, Sasha," Cooper whined.

"Me too," admitted Sasha, "but don't worry. Casey will be able to clear her name. I'm sure of it." She tried to sound as encouraging as possible, but she knew that Juniper was on the verge of successfully ousting his biggest obstacle to the war. She caught glimpses of him whimpering some soft commands to the canine military ranks. Sasha laid down, resting her head on her paws, and sighed. "Casey, please hurry," she thought to herself.

LITTLE AND MANY PAWS AND CLAWS

I t was late evening by the time Casey trotted back with Representative Lucky to his base, where she had first encountered the fananas. The neighborhood seemed unchanged from her first visit. They squeezed through the wooden fence, and Casey found herself in the small triangular back yard with the now quiet woods in the back of them. The house stood ominously quiet, its white paint chipping all along the length of its three stories. The back porch of the house creaked in the wind, and the lattice covering the area under the porch seemed somehow different than the last time she had seen it. What it was, though, she could not place her paw on.

Lucky sat back on his haunches, "I asked the two dogs with the information to appear here in about a half hour's time. We just need to wait a bit," he said, looking around as if worried someone might hear. "Can I ask you something, Senator?"

Casey looked to the woods, confirming their silence, and then back along the length of the yard. "Sure, Representative. To be sure, I'm glad that you approached me, although I hope I can help you as much as you hope to be helped."

"What do you feel is the endpoint of our situation?"

"Whose situation? Endpoint? I'm not sure I understand."

"The Central Canine Government. Surely you know that no species can maintain any civilization indefinitely. Even the humans are thought to fail more than they succeed."

"Well," mused Casey, her whiskers flickering thoughtfully, "I don't think our government or our civilization is in any immediate danger. Even in the current conflict with the Wilds, we will likely remain intact, if changed a bit. I don't think that the way of the Wilds is sustainable. The loose associations and mercenary mentality leaves too many pups by the wayside. I think we will go on as long as I'm alive."

"But that's not a long time," Lucky seemed almost to be scoffing at her, "and you're also assuming that canines themselves are largely responsible for their own position in this world."

"Well, who else would be responsible?" Casey thought she saw something moving out of the corner of her eye towards the house. She stared for several seconds and concluded that all was quiet.

This time Lucky obviously scoffed in his response, "The humans, Senator, the humans. If it was not for them, we would be nothing and would enjoy no luxuries."

"I assure you that they would be as lost without us as we would be without them. It is because of the way we have endeared the humans to us that we have been so successful, Representative Lucky. Surely, the humans are not so powerful that we need to be constantly concerned about staying in their good graces? If that were so, we would not have to worry about the fananas or the Wilds, since the humans would be able to keep them from us at all times, not to mention force us to come snout-to-snout with the notion that we have no power at all."

"Or that we have only as much power as the humans decide to give us, and that they do not *protect* us because they do not care to."

A rustling. Casey turned sharply. She was sure she saw something stirring, as if the house itself was coming alive. "Lucky, did you see something?"

Lucky had been continuing to pontificate, "...and I guess that's why I sought their counsel first, as a means to an end, but then it turned into something larger."

"Wait, what are you barking about?"

"My friends, my allies. Ones whom I can trust exactly because they have thought about the larger role of their own species in ways that most canines cannot comprehend." Lucky shifted his eyes away from the house as if trying to ignore it.

"There are no other dogs with any such information about Juniper," Casey whimpered.

The latticework below the porch creaked. Black, shining eyes peered out from the gaps in the wood, and a flash of brown fur started to peek out from each hole.

"You see, Senator Casey, you are so worried about Juniper and the Wilds and war that you fail to identify the real problem."

As if signaled, small little noses with brown bodies and long leathery tails poured from the latticework below the porch like water over the edge of a cliff. From top to bottom, the porch spewed rats of all colors and shapes and sizes. Casey instinctively backed up slowly, mechanically. The rats advanced towards Casey with an almost mindless purpose. Casey could hear the scuffling of all the tiny paws against the ground as the smell of the foul tide enveloped the yard. Lucky barked furiously from the far edge of the lawn. "We have successfully recruited all sorts of dogs and mice and rats from every sector, Senator. Once my friends have taken care of you, I can easily blame Juniper and all his ilk. With the obvious failure and corruption of the Central Canine Government, canines everywhere will be desperate for a way out of the two-front battle between the fananas and the Wilds. Then I will propose a radical concept: ally with the ones we previously abhorred and find true freedom in our strength in numbers. We would no longer have to depend on humans for food, sustenance, housing, protection. We will be our own protectors."

Casey was backed up against the chain-link fence, nearly fifty yards deep from the far edges of the lawn. A brown and black sea of vermin covered the entire expanse. The chain-link fence was too high for her to leap, and she was sure that the lead rats were laughing at her fear. Casey pushed the bulk of her body weight against the fence and, in doing so, stirred up a bit of dirt beneath her hind paws.

Digging!!

It was the only way out. With Labrador intensity, she planted her hind legs and flung dirt from the edge of the fence. The rats were coming on quickly, about twenty yards away. Right away, Casey could see that the lower edge of the fence was barely an inch buried, and within a few seconds, a small hole was emerging from her work.

The wave of vermin closed quickly. Casey looked down—there was no way she could get her body through the hole. She barked, showing teeth to stave off the rats. The front of the wave paused but was soon shoved forward by the weight of the tide. She tested the hole. No good. Dirt flew around her, covering her face, legs, and paws. The rats were a dog's length away. Casey whimpered, anticipating the impact.

Howling filled the air. The tide paused, but resurged again. A second time, more distinct—a raspy, energetic howl. Casey looked over at the entrance from the wooden fence where she came in and a head poked through. It was Chuckles. From every single direction, instantaneously and in pairs, two dozen Rat Terriers threw themselves into the wave. They were mostly white with scattered black, and they converged on the mass of rats like flame engulfs tinder. Two on either side of Casey leapt from the other side of the fence. Casey could not believe that she did not see the Rat Terriers coming in from the woods. The rats frantically oriented and re-oriented to take on the assailants. Chuckles sidled up besides Casey, watching the action. Two pairs of Rat Terriers trotted up behind him, growling protectively.

"Special forces Rat Terrier squad was very upset to hear about this," he quipped.

Casey marveled at the unmatched speed of the squad. The two pairs of Rat Terriers that flanked her dispatched the vermin with alarming speed. They moved steadily forward, flashing their teeth. In between growls and barks, injured and dead rats flew in every direction. At length, a white Terrier turned to Casey.

"Senator, we can mop up this mess from here on. There's an alternate route that bypasses Lucky's personal security squads, especially that creepy orange wanyamas that a few of us passed going in. If you go along the far edge of the chain-link fence where it meets that wooden fence, the edge of it is free and turns up. You can nose your way through, and Senator Chuckles knows the rest of the way."

"What are you going to do with Lucky?"

The Rat Terrier squad leader smiled, and her tongue flicked out along the left edge of her snout. "A debriefing...of sorts."

Casey thanked the squad leader and looked around the yard. More than three quarters of the rats lay dead or injured. Two of the smaller squad members had pulled back the latticework attached to the porch and were systematically exterminating the remainder. As Casey slipped into the woods with Chuckles in tow, she caught a glimpse of the tails of two squad members, disappearing excitedly into the darkness of the porch.

THUNDER

Casey knew where they were headed: to get home, they had to skirt a portion of the downtown area, which was dominated by the Wilds. Casey knew that populous territory devoid of greenery lay ahead, although she was unsure of the exact boundaries of the woods. She was grateful to Chuckles for saving her, despite his recent betrayal. In the back of her mind, she feared that the fananas lurked somewhere in the dense forest.

The day wore into night, and as the sunlight waned, a grey mist wove in and around the higher brush on the forest floor, dancing around the dogs' legs. Casey paused at intervals, looking back for Chuckles, who had a hard time keeping pace because of his shorter legs. Almost in spite of herself, Casey appreciated his emergence from the soupy mist.

They got to talking about routine goings-on, and eventually the conversation wore down to the present situation. "Casey," Chuckles said, attempting to bore into her thoughts, "what are we going to do if this comes to open conflict? I don't think that with everything going on, the government can survive such an ordeal. Surely, the Wilds have, at least in theory, greater resources at their disposal?"

"Well, now we know that Lucky had an agenda. We have always known Juniper's agenda, and we assume that we know the Wilds' agenda. We're about out of agendas to discover! If we can get back in time, we might be able to derail a full-on preemptive assault. Even the suspicion of impropriety might be enough to force a Hold of Government vote."[16]

16 The Hold of Government Act was a separate bill immediately following the initial Canine Constitution. The sole aim of the motion was to put a halt on any bills or actions just ratified by Congress in the most recent seven days. It also forces all canines to report to a pre-determined central area or send a delegate representative to re-visit all threatened bills. The bill was hastily passed after the Constitution was created as a means to prevent hastily passed misguided legislation. The only caveat of the Hold of Government Act is that it has a "new information" requirement whereby a threatened bill can only be completely repealed if a member of Congress has two independent witnesses with verifiable new information not previously known and/or direct evidence also not previously known.

"We still have no clear idea what the fananas' role in all of this is."

"What if they have no role? What if their presence is coincidental, or a by-product of something else?"

Chuckles snorted loudly, "Not likely. We have had an uneventful period for years and then everything erupts. We're on the verge of war, you might get ousted from your seat, and the Contrarians will lose the government."

They lapsed into silence as they walked. Casey's mind drifted. Then, she stopped suddenly.

"How could we have betrayed them?"

Chuckles stepped alongside her. "Who?"

"The Yorkies. When I went to go talk to the birds, a crow intercepted us and told us that the Yorkies are not lost, but left because they were betrayed by the canines. But how? Sure, we have lots of influence on where various litters are deployed and how the neighborhoods are patrolled, but there is a lot of freedom instilled in our system. I just don't see how we might have forced those dogs out."

Chuckles shook his head and kept walking. The sun finally dipped down below the recognizable horizon, and a silence emerged from the infrequent chatter of the surrounding forest. There were no notable human structures in sight.

The two dogs assumed a closer posture. Casey paused more and more frequently as she sniffed the ground. Finally she came to a stop.

"Ok Chuckles, I am not sure where to go. I'm getting mixed scentimas. Several are telling me that only a few hundred yards down that way to the left is the outskirts of the Wilds territory. Other scentimas are telling me that the forest stretches on for days. What do you think we should do?"

"Plow forward to the edge of the Wilds and back to Canine Government controlled land. We need to keep moving—I just received word that there's thunder behind us, and that a storm is bearing down."

"Storm?" Casey replied, shocked, "The overwhelming amount of scentimas has never failed to notify us before a storm. We would have known earlier today, with the sun high in the sky. How could we have missed it? Are you sure you did not misinterpret the scentima?"

Chuckles gave a pensive look to the right and then an even more hesitant reply, "Well, it said 'thunderous' then STOP, and 'beware a storm' then STOP."[17]

"Curious," Casey whimpered. She picked her steps carefully in the growing darkness. Chuckles needed to double-time his steps every ten to fifteen feet to keep pace with the husky Labrador.

She turned to allow Chuckles to catch up, when she heard a rumbling coming from somewhere behind them.

"Thunder...?" whimpered Chuckles, as if pleading to Casey to let it be so.

Casey tilted her snout up in the air and drank in as much information as she could. "Mixed scentimas. There's a lot of misdirection in the air today. But that's NOT thunder."

The rumbling came from another direction, this one seeming a little farther off. Before they could react, the first disturbance re-emerged, blending with the second and slowly fading.

Casey had a brief vision of a huge pack of fananas bearing down on them and shuddered. The canine authorities had no idea where they were, and there were no humans for miles. The two rumbles sounded again, lasting longer this time, coupled closely together. Casey's instinct took over. "Chuckles," Casey's bark stern and measured, "we had better run as fast as we can, towards where we think human civilization might be. Whatever that is, it's coming right at us."

---

17 Scentimas were transmitted most often in fragments and required an understanding of the context for interpretation. The canines readily recognized the pitfalls of the scentimas, but lack of more sophisticated manners of communication available precluded them from abandoning the practice. To combat it, the Scentima Redundancy Act was passed requiring all official government-designated scentima couriers to deliver scentimas in pairs. Because scentimas were olfactory footprints, they differed slightly and subtly even if obtained at the same time, and the interpretable information from the two were often complementary to one another. This act, however, only covered scentimas delivered under certain conditions by government-designated couriers, and there was a lot of unofficial, unverifiable information traversing canine territory all the time.

With that, the two took off through the woods at breakneck speed. Unlike cats, they could not run silently, and the brush and branches tore away at the pounding of their paws. Casey could not help but cringe at the noise they made, but the rumbling was rapidly descending upon them, and she soon discarded the thought.

The forest seemed endless, and tree after tree gave way only to more of the same. Chuckles fell behind her, and Casey turned at intervals, whimpering to urge him onwards. "I'm trying, I'm trying!! A little tough when I'm literally a fifth of your size!!" Chuckles barked back, more out of fear than indignation.

The rumbling gained. "It's like they're sending an army after us." Casey thought to herself. She imagined a horde of fananas, fangs bared, galloping towards her. Just as it seemed the pursuers were on top of them, Casey and Chuckles came up to the edge of a hilltop with a gradual slope that fed out into an ordered set of trees, all bearing fruit. Beyond this grove, Casey could see a house. Relief! She pulled up to a slow trot near the edge of the hilltop and turned to see if Chuckles had caught up, but the darkness would not yield him. Casey could not pick out the gentler padding of his paws beyond the heavy thuds of the pursuing herd.

The rumbling halted. Casey could see the black curtain of the forest now. Three dark, hulking shapes pulled up to a walk just before the edge of the forest. Casey could hear their heavy panting, and as they emerged, she saw the grey coloration of their coats.

Her hair instinctively stood up along her spine, and she gave a halfway glance to the house at the far end of the orchard. She knew she could not outrun these three. She barked nervously and loud, but with a tinge of desperation. "What do you want with me?!"

"For you to come with us, Senator," a familiar voice sounded. Three Greyhound couriers emerged with a happy Chuckles dancing around and between their legs.

"There's been a governmental crisis, Casey."

Relief robbed Casey of her thoughts. Recovering, she stammered,

"But there's three of you. Has PupCon One been declared?"[18]

"It has, Senator," responded the lead Greyhound. "My name is Wicket, and we've come to escort you back to the dog park, where the remainder of the senators and representatives have gathered. I can brief you on the essential facts that I have been made privy to, but you will no doubt have more questions than I have answers."

Both Chuckles and Casey exchanged a glance. "Have we been attacked?"

A pause. The Greyhounds were all still panting heavily from their run. "No *confirmed* attack has occurred. The Senate is deadlocked on a bill, and President Darma pro-offered an unorthodox method to resolve it. Members of your committee challenged her right to do so, and the entire Committee for Defense challenged *their* rights to oppose it. Senator Cooper then demanded that a Dominance match ensue between himself and Juniper. Before it could take place, the majority of Submissivist representatives stormed the Senate floor and demanded that the bill be passed. They had the votes to ratify it. The meeting went into chaos. Unofficial Dominance matches began to occur, and the Bulldog Police had to be called in. President Darma has demanded that PupCon One be declared only because she received a message that the Wilds had breached the perimeter."

"You said we weren't being attacked?"

"We're not. At least not yet. The Wilds declared to all dogs in the territory they entered that they were laying claim to that neighborhood. The canine citizens acquiesced, and the local officials were routed. It's clear that other neighborhoods are considering seceding from the government to join the Wilds."

"The problems continue to compound," barked Casey. "Our greatest problem is becoming ourselves. At this point, the Wilds and

18 PupCon also referred to as Puppy Condition was a euphemism for the state of the government in relation to war or crisis. PupCon Three was peace and One was either war or an equivalent crisis that threatened the government's existence. Whatever the cause of the crisis, the bylaws specifically required that three Greyhound couriers must seek out any government officials not at their home base. The reason for three of them was thought to be because of concern for being attacked, and three was considered a "safe amount" for alerting to the attack or crisis and assumed that, of three Greyhounds, at least one would likely be speedy enough to get away to the government officials.

fananas are going to be encroaching on a government in shambles. The lawlessness will spread, and no canine will be safe."

Wicket nodded and pointed with his snout. "We can cut through this peach grove, then a right to the north, and we'll come back around to the northern-most edge of your territory, Senator Casey. We can have you back within a few hours."

"Lead the way, couriers." Casey and Chuckles sighed a mixture of relief and growing anxiety. The Greyhounds tore down the slope at nearly blurring speed, and Chuckles whimpered a bit as he and Casey followed them. They got down the slope quickly, and Casey barked for them to slow down. A quick look back by Wicket followed by some short, sporadic barks to slow down had the Greyhounds slow to an effortless gallop, while Casey ran and Chuckles sprinted to keep up. The group of five dogs angled around the trees, weaving serpentine around them. Chuckles was not sure he could keep pace. Near the edge of the grove as it yielded to an open field, Casey saw the trio of Greyhounds take a hard right followed by a quick hard left, as if dodging something. The field looked clear, thought Casey to herself, and she decided to plow straight ahead. As she neared where they had weaved, the rear Greyhound yipped excitedly, "Senator, there's an obscured hole—"

It was too late. Casey gave a yelp as the ground disappeared from underneath her paws. She slid down a muddy, wet hole, over twelve feet deep. Casey came to a stop near a small rivulet at the bottom. She was covered from head to paw in thick, wet mud. It took her eyes a moment to adjust, but she could see that the rivulet came from a series of tunnels ahead of her, and that damp light bathed the walls down one particular direction.

"Casey!" Chuckles and the Greyhounds barked in unison down the hole.

"I'm here, and I'm fine," she barked back. "It seems like a maze down here. There's some light off to one direction. I'll follow it out."

Wicket clearly nervous, barked, "Senator Casey, what would you like us to do? Should we fetch human-mates?" Casey could hear them whimpering above her.

"The water is coming from somewhere, Wicket. I'll follow it out and then send some scentimas around so you can home in on my location."

"We'll send some more Greyhounds out to cover more territory, Senator. We'll need to get you back quickly before the crisis extends!" Casey heard them thundering away, and very quickly, she was alone. She swished along the rivulet, and her paw pads hit the water with a slap at each step. She advanced along the tunnel a few hundred yards, and her stomach fell. There was a five-way intersection, and the faint light came not from outside, but from semi-luminescent crystals embedded in the rock walls. Casey heaved an exasperated sigh before trudging along the rivulet's path, hoping she was heading along in the same direction that the Greyhounds had told her would lead back home. She had plodded through the water for nearly an hour when the crystals became more prevalent, and the tunnel shone brighter and brighter. Casey stopped, peering closely at this new phenomenon, until she was suddenly aware of a new odor creeping around her, only barely familiar.

A voice with a thick accent pierced her thinking, "Well, what do we have here?"

The muddy, drenched Casey turned her head and whimpered fearfully. Rats, innumerable and each twice the size of those seen in Lucky's back yard, measured her silently.

"How could any of those Greyhounds know my location?" Casey thought to herself.

WILDS ON THE WAY

"The strategy is simple," the lean, shrewd Madison proclaimed to a crowded subway entrance on the outskirts of the city, "we need to interrupt the flow of two things that the Central Canine Government holds so dear."

"What would those two be?" oozed Asher, the ratty grey and white alley cat.

"Communication and puppy dispersal. The communication is easy, but they will recover quickly. The flow of puppies to various neighborhoods is the Central Government's only means of control. If they like how you govern your territory, more puppies are allocated to your neighborhood. If you're less important, you get less puppies. In addition, each area gets educational support for the puppies that they garner, so the richer neighborhoods have more resources, and the poorer ones can never catch up. It is an unsustainable system, and we can exploit those weaknesses."

"I don't understand why a full-scale invasion would not be wiser," piped up a small Corgie mix. "We know they're reeling, and the emergence of the fananas is weakening the base of both parties. There's general unrest. We know that their famed leader of defense, Juniper, does not have the muscle to combat even a quarter of all the dog and catpower we have at our disposal."

"You forget," Madison chastised, "the one thing that keeps the masses of the Central Canine Government clinging to their officials is the promise and occasional show of force should there be an invasion. They talk of 'carambee,' and it pervades the educational experience of the puppies, all of which are indoctrinated into this false ideology. If we launch a full-scale invasion, we reinforce that tenuous link between all of those loosely associated factions that want to oppose the government. In fact, the same leaders of those various factions are praying that we not do not invade, lest they lose their hold on whatever group they are brainwashing. One group boasts that the main issue is bringing forth religion from the zealots into government, that the 'godlessness' of the government is to blame, and the fananas are 'devils' sent by some maker. Another group claims that the immigration of mixed breed dogs threatens their 'way of life' and that there are not enough resources to sustain all dogs, finite number of humans, that kind of stuff. They are all barking around the issues but forget to see the real problem: Canine Congress itself. The Canine Congress only exists for itself. They have evolved to a point where the lead officials control enough infrastructure that they can create for their own neighborhood the life they like, fashion a bond with the humans in ways that they see fit, and they get to make decisions for other dogs that could likely do so for themselves if it was not for the fear that drives them to rely on these senators, representatives, and their joke of a President, Darma. Years ago, there may have been more danger, but there was more of what we know now is important, *huria*, and now the fools are so entrenched with their own government that cutting those ties without backup would be like throwing them to the fananas."

"And what of the fananas, Madison?" Asher posed herself, "What do we do about them? What if they decide to ruin our little coup?" Asher, despite her allegiance to Madison's authority, had no qualms about challenging her authority on any matter, even in mixed company, before inferiors and superiors.

Madison licked her muzzle pensively. "Well, we cannot worry about them now. Until a few days ago, they were only legends, and we don't know where they came from, why they are here, or what they want. We forge ahead with our plan, and, if everything goes as planned, we'll have so much strength of numbers, the fananas would be wise to respect our boundaries."

A general cacophony of throaty growls and low barks briefly interrupted the meeting. They were into the fourth hour of debate. Madison had entered the meeting with a strategy to at least stop the likely onslaught of violence that the dogs of larger territories were aiming for. EastandMain, however, a wiry Boxer mix who presided over the largest number of blocks, surprised her and opposed those that pushed for an outright attack. EastandMain stood up; he had been lying down, seemingly oblivious to most of the discussions of the meeting. He emitted his distinctive baritone growl, and all ears and eyes turned to acknowledge him.

"I know most of you are hesitant about accepting Madison's plan. I can also understand why you doubt that it will work. To sit idly by, however, and plan the attack of a century, only to wait for some theoretical point in time where the Canine Government has reached maximum vulnerability, is akin to chasing puppy dreams. For too long we have harbored anger and disgust for those that are within the realm of that ridiculous government. We need to think of that government's constituents, who are victims of the CCG. Perhaps offering liberation is a better option than conquering them. After all, if you truly value huria in your canine hearts, then you would want it for all."

A heavy silence hung across the array of dogs. Some sat and stared, seeming barely to breathe. Others thoughtfully scratched an ear or shifted their gaze anxiously as they took in the whole of the statement. Madison broke the reverie first, "We leave in the morning. We canvas the entire border of West-town, and, if our intelligence is accurate, the remainder of West-town will go along with the border neighborhoods. Once word of the 'change of management' gets around, East-town and South-town should be amenable to negotiations. The central territory and North-town will be holdouts, but, by that time, their Congress will be totally destabilized, and, while they are busy arranging attacks and counting tails, we'll move with local civilian forces to intercept the Bulldog Police. They'll be out-pawed and will have no choice but to surrender under new rule." Madison barked out the last phrase with enough gusto to get them all standing. "Now..." she continued, "any questions?"

One usually meek Chow mix whimpered a timid reply, "What if our intelligence is inaccurate and we get there only to meet heavy resistance from our rule?"

The two most militant dogs stepped confidently forward. Division, a beefy German Shepherd, and Orchard, a fiery Irish Setter mix, nodded to both Madison and EastandMain.

Madison paused briefly, and EastandMain stalwartly barked

with a tinny voice, "Then..." he oozed, sweeping his gaze across the assembly, "then, we force them."

With that, the animals exploded in lusty celebration. The meeting broke soon afterwards.

"I agree with you, Madison," Asher hissed at her, following quickly at her heels, "but the noble quest of a nonhostile takeover is doomed to fail. It will come to violence."

"I have one more idea," Madison replied. "You didn't think I would show my entire paw only to allow this whole affair to come to war, did you?"

Asher mewed laughter. "What do you have in mind?"

"When your compatriots become foes," Madison barked, "you need new allies."

HATRED AND HISTORY

C asey's fur was near perpendicular to her skin along the entire length of her back, and even her flanks were puffed up to porcupine proportions. Water came up just past her dewclaw, and it had a stale, stagnant odor although it continued to flow. Casey continued to step forward slowly despite recognizing she was clearly surrounded. She could see plenty of eyes, numerous rat faces, but they were all motionless. Deep in the background, possibly to parallel tunnels, she could hear an occasional scrape. The odor was nearly impenetrable by any scentimas which also helped her to continue to pad forward, as standing still seemed to make the smells weigh on her further. The voice, clearly in Domesticated Common, that had harkened Casey to the rat's presence, repeated a question this time, "Canine, why have you come to us?"

This time she paused, "By accident," Casey said. "I have no argument with any of you … rats."

"Welllll, that's interesting," a large rat stepped carefully in front of Casey, "because we've heard that salutation before, only to find the speaker meant otherwise. We know these tunnels very well, though, and I know that there is an easily accessible entrance near here. I'm inclined to think you fell in. Kind of fortuitous, I would say."

"Why is that," Casey barked nervously, "because you have me outnumbered?"

"Ha! Pup, just because we can does not always mean we do. We operate by strength of numbers mainly for organization's sake. Taking down large animals such as yourself would not be, well, prudent, and we Norway rats are always prudent."

"Then just let me pass. I'll be quick about finding my way out."

A general hub-ub of activity sounded around the lead rat and echoed against the tunnel walls. The trickling water rushed around Casey's paws, and she backpedaled: the rats were too close for comfort. She realized that the tunnels must be wider than she had thought. The blackness she had mistaken for the boundaries of the tunnel melted away when the rats advanced from the shadows. Like an illusion, Casey thought to herself.

"We can show you out, if you wouldn't mind filling us in on a few details," the large lead rat offered.

Casey whimpered a bit. The incident in Lucky's yard was fresh in her mind. "I really don't mind. I just need to be shown the general direction—"

"Don't trust us, eh?"

"It's not that—"

"I think I get it. You see, my friend of the canine persuasion, we are well aware of our role in the world. You, no doubt, have been exposed to rats before—"

"I had a recent run-in with your kind on the surface. If it wasn't for some of my more militant friends, I might have been half-devoured by now."

"Ugh. Roof rats, always ruining things for the rest of us."

"What?"

The lead rat hopped onto a small ledge that bordered the central depression of the tunnel. Casey thought she could see a bit of dog in him as he sort of half-circled before he laid down and peered at Casey with deep, black eyes, "The roof rats are the rogue subspecies that even we dread. They seem unassuming compared to us, as you can see, because we are nearly twice the size of them. We have found it nearly intolerable to be near them."

"Why?" Casey could not believe she was getting mired into the political details of the nameless vermin. Surely, her journey had taken her well beyond the normal comfort zone for any canine.

"They talk about the intolerance of other animals to 'our kind' without recognizing their own shortcomings. They're religious fanatics. The god that most rats worship is named Panya. It is the great Panya that oversees us all, but the roof rats have brought it to a higher level. A subsect of the roof rats that found religion particularly important legislated that Panya could not be spoken of by name at any point. Ridiculous! One can't discuss this notion with the roof rats, either, because it inevitably leads to the name of our god being said, and, at that point, we become heretics to them and are therefore too offensive to discuss anything with. They were the first ones to claim that anyone and everyone was intolerant to their religious views, and yet, they displayed an incredible amount of intolerance in the presentation of their religion."

"Well, my rat friend, I could not start to understand the complex nature of your—"

"Listening is clearly not a strong point for canines, is it? Do you realize that you're at a cross-roads in your own evolution?"

The silence of the tunnel was broken by the occasional sounds of the water. It was difficult for Casey to wrap her mind around these rats that inexplicably spoke her language and seemed markedly presumptuous as well. "Listen—"

"Call me Friedwarf."

"Friedwarf, I am not going to go into the details of canine politics, but I must get back to my kind. There is an emergency, and I am needed."

"I know. You're trying to resolve the conflict between your group and the untamed dogs that live in the city."

"Well, yes, but—"

"All the while trying to reconcile the appearance of vicious, dog-like animals that are encroaching upon your territory?"

"How do you know this?"

"Do you know what Norway rats do?"

Casey increasingly felt like her control was being wrested from her grip. "No," she said.

"We are the historians of the animal world. You see, canine, we have logged in our own long, sad history in efforts to shed light on our miserable existence and, we hope, to bring us to a time when more of our kind, as well as others, can share in the wealth of human existence."

Casey felt fluffed up by this statement. How could a rat know what it meant to be endeared to the human-mates? Surely, they were delusional if they thought that the human-mates could ever think more of them than the canines.

"I can tell you feel that our knowledge of the humans is unlikely, but let us show you something."

With that, Casey heard a scurrying all around her. Suddenly, the entire tunnel was flooded with light. Casey saw that she was walking in a central canal with ledges about four feet deep on either side. The entire corridor was flooded with rats, so much so that they almost seemed to be standing on top of one another. The light reflected off of the walls, upon which innumerable things had been written. "What is that stuff?" Casey barked. She could not read it, and it was clearly in the rats' native language.

"The events of many generations. Only by chronicling all of our misfortunes could we start to understand them. Do you know how endeared to humanity rats once were?"

Casey snorted with laughter, her tail wagged sarcastically in response. She barked back patronizingly, "Go ahead, my rat friend, tell me how much the humans valued you."

There was a scurrying behind Friedwarf. "I assure you, it's true. Many years ago, long before dogs were even important to people, the humans lived difficult lives. The most dangerous enemy that any human encountered was other humans. The humans lived by farming crops in the field, and it was only through many years of infighting and organizing and disorganizing and then re-organizing, that they started to form into little groups for the purpose of safety. They then established rules among themselves to aid in self-governance. For the first time in hundreds of years, which spanned hundreds of our generations and would be like dozens of yours, they lived in close proximity to one another. Today, we take this for granted. We see humans walking alongside one another, and it looks and seems normal, but there was a time when that closeness equaled danger. So the city was born. The humans reveled in their accomplishment, and, in many ways, we rats celebrated with them. We fed on grain when they worked in farms, and in the cities, we grew fat off the multitude of things they discarded. Sure, from time to time, they let a cat loose on us, but, by and large, the humans saw us as a tolerable nuisance."

Casey could see the looks of admiration that the rats bestowed upon their leader. On the walls, there were annotations in Domesticated Common, sparse though they were, that a lean rat wrote as the leader spoke. Slowly, the language of the inscriptions came into a bit of focus, although Casey could not appreciate it all.

"...then the disease came..."

"Disease?" The story was suddenly intriguing.

"We had seen a human become sick and even die, but this was unlike anything we had ever seen. Suddenly, large quantities of humans became bedridden, and many were dying. Bodies of humans began to pile up in the cities. The humans resorted to bizarre things to ward off the disease. We discovered that it became only a matter of time..."

"Matter of time before what?"

"Before we were blamed."

"But, but why?"

Friedwarf's nose flickered back and forth. Suddenly it struck Casey how out of proportion the volume of the lead rat's voice was in comparison with his size. Friedwarf laughed before responding, "Humans are tremendously complex, puppy. Their achievements on this wide world dwarf any of ours in comparison, but they also have a tremendous ability to find fault with other groups for all of their problems, even when the problems that occur are primarily a result of their own actions. Hence, the rats eventually became blamed for the Great Plague. We obviously cannot understand all details of the human language, but there are many theories about how we came to become targets of their wrath."

The darkness and the stench of the tunnels melted away as Casey became engrossed in the story, "We are far more endeared to the humans than your kind, surely, we don't really know of the wrath you speak of."

Friedwarf shook with sarcasm, "Listen more, dog, and I will then show you firsthand of the wrath of the humans. For years leading up to the plague, we rejoiced in the tolerance of humans. Once they became adept at building and residing in cities, the struggles of their existence became less of a struggle. Flour and cornmeal accumulated, and we ate off of the excess of the humans. We were bothersome but not dangerous. Through the plague, we persevered and were unaware of the magnitude of the events that would follow.

Then, traps appeared, and poisoned food. One rat would arrive to a den, and a day later, ninety percent of the family was wiped out. Cats had always been a problem, but dogs and other animals were soon trained just to trap and kill us. Homes became increasingly difficult to penetrate. Even as we preferred to be ignored, we were targeted. The prevailing theory is that humans think *we* gave them the disease that killed so many. When the surface became unlivable, we learned to tunnel and build cities of our own. Far more limited than humans in ability, we began to study why it was that humans, of all the species on the planet, excelled and dominated. They are slower than most and are weak compared to large predators. One large dog could make multiple humans cower before it. For years, we toiled and studied and collected information, all while struggling mightily to survive. As we collected the knowledge, we gradually devised a way to chronicle it, so that future generations would not have to start over. Several generations of our kind come and go even with just one of yours. It was not until we felt we had exhausted so many possibilities that we realized the answer to human dominance was literally just before our paws and noses, and now, before yours."

Casey looked around, baffled, as Friedwarf smiled at her, "So... what is it?" Friedwarf chuckled. "What? I cannot read it, rat. Look, if you want to make me look foolish."

"No, dog. You don't need to be able to read our language. It is the chronicling of things that is the source of their strength. They build knowledge over large quantities of time, and nothing becomes lost. If one human fails while building a wall, the second comes by and reads the ways in which the first faltered and completes that wall. An incredible system, one designed by a creature with so many weaknesses, so many faults, and so slow to learn. Absolutely ingenious, and, now, we are also on our way."

Casey sniffed at the vast writings on the wall, looking at the rat historians as she passed. Several rats would stop by at one point or another and make small etchings, as if making corrections or adjustments or, sometimes, to reinforce that which was already written. Casey was not sure if rats sighed, but she felt that Friedwarf was sighing out of awe as she saw his whiskers were not twitching as rapidly as he too peered at the wall.

Casey thought briefly of the Squirrel Report and what a wonder it might be if they collected the information. She whimpered, softly, "We have never thought of doing such things. We have the Reciting Barkers, but I never thought of ..."

Friedwarf seemed to pity her "The truth is, dog, that you canines are too self-centered to have thought of such things. Such invention requires a sense of one's place within the species and the thought of the species' place within the world. You have paralleled the humans in that respect. They are unconscionably self-centered."

"Now, wait," Casey barked back, "the tenets of our laws and of the foundations of canine religions speak often of the love shared by humans and dogs. We have helped the humans as they have us, which only generated more love and compassion."

The rat seemed to shrug nonexistent shoulders, "You mistake reliance for love. As humans excelled at dominating animals, they turned their eyes towards some for companionship as well as work. Hence, canines. Dogs attached themselves and their destinies to humans when they saw that the food train never ran on empty. Various stories cropped up to explain a sudden realization that dogs were wholly in the midst of humans, but only a few thought to question how they came to be. Other, craftier dogs laid in wait for those asking the questions. They had elaborate and sometimes fantastical answers, and so religion, customs, and canine government was born." Friedwarf gestured to a particular section of a tunnel as they made their way along the several corridors. As he told the story, he gestured towards the etchings in front of him as he often looked to them for referral, or else it was indicative of some rat-like pride.

"I have never heard of such nonsense."

"Do you know how the laws that you have came to be?"

He had Casey there. "I...don't know the origin, not exactly," Casey stammered hastily. "Our laws are present because we know them, and all canines recite them once elected, and the Reciting Barkers keep the more relevant laws fresh in our minds. They are also taught to the puppies as they are trained and prior to their dispersal."

"What happens if something is forgotten? Are there laws that are forgotten?" The rat did not seem to know, but his whiskers twitched curiously, drinking in any response from the Labrador senator.

"I guess some laws have been forgotten, but how could they then have been important? We keep that which is most important on our mind, and our civilization has swelled as a result."

"Interesting," Friedwarf did not elaborate further, "I suppose it's a fairly sustainable system in the short term. I doubt even the wolves have concocted anything that sophisticated."

"Wolves?"

"Ahhh," Friedwarf scurried over to another mural of writings, "I think you call them fananas, your predecessors. They came before you, and, gradually, all dogs have hailed from them."

Casey could barely contain her mirth, "Listen, rat. I have heard similar claims from the felines. With all the variety with breeds, it's surely ridiculous that we would all come from the same animals. I am not in the practice of believing in magic."

"I don't dispute you that it sounds odd, dog. But the truth is, I trust the documentation from all the rats that have come before me. I am Friedwarf the 703rd, and though not all Friedwarfs have served consecutively, we all have standards for our historical documents that are followed to the letter. There is some dispute among our theorists about how this all happened, but it's clearly spelled out that many, many generations ago, wolves were occasionally kept by humans, and only a few generations hence the dogs appeared. In our scientific classes, we talk about the possibility that changes occur in entire species of animals, such as dogs, over time, and given a push by the humans for change. Some of our more religious brethren, such as the roof rats, argue that Panya created dogs separate from the wolves, or the fananas, because it simply does not make sense that such variety stemmed from one source. I have stressed that it's ok whatever one rat wants to think about how other animals came to be, but that the facts cannot be disputed. Personally speaking, the religious view cannot be taught side by side with the science because it distorts the strict adherence to the methods for the science we are attempting to instill. Anyway, there were only fananas at one time, but then there were dogs and fananas."

The vivacity of Friedwarf's explanation almost seemed to transform for Casey some of the unintelligible writings. There were some crude pictorial descriptions interspersed in the record that Casey could loosely follow. It made a sort of sense, yet she remained intensely skeptical of their anti-human stance.

"The thing we cannot figure out, dog," Friedwarf went on, "is why your committee leader for canine defense pursues his declaration of war and then allies himself with another dog who was attempting to betray the entire canine species?"

Did Juniper know Lucky was a traitor, or did he simply miscalculate? Casey assumed that the rats' vast intelligence network had led Friedwarf to his conclusion. She now knew that the rats enjoyed their role as historians, and so had no real designs to achieve dominion over other animals. She continued to study the writings, although she comprehended little. There was so much information before her that she could spend days taking it all in. She noticed some pictures of humans with some bizarre objects. Her own personal human-mates had some things that she thought might be similar.

"Friedwarf, my rat friend," Casey gently barked, "what do these pictures show?"

"Ahhhh, the humans' inventions. Like the humans, these have multiplied greatly over only our last thirty or so generations. Some are large, while others are very small. They populate the human world in ever increasing numbers."

"And you say that the humans are more self-centered than the canines?"

"At least in our estimation."

"The religious zealots talk about a void that we filled. Our role in their world was to aid in teaching them about love and companionship. Each of the major canine religions has a different idea about how and why these came to be, but, before us, humans existed, and without us, clearly they would continue..."

Friedwarf's whiskers flickered in thought, "That makes sense, given what we know."

"Maybe Juniper knew and was banking on the betrayal. He *wanted* to disrupt the entire canine society. I think he thinks those *inventions* have taken the humans from us. Those objects, their focus of attention *might* be doing that, but since we are all still well taken care of, he's prematurely upsetting the balance."

Friedwarf had led Casey as they talked. Casey cocked her head at Friedwarf when she saw that an offshoot of the tunnel led outside into a muddy expanse. It was rainy and dark outside, but Casey could make out some cages maybe fifty feet from the tunnel, maybe a dozen or so. She could make out the outline of animals lying still in the dark with the rain bearing down. "What is this?" Casey quietly whimpered to Friedwarf.

Friedwarf did not meet Casey's gaze with his own, "Take a look, my canine friend, and see what the humans have done, but be quick: there are evil humans near."

The heavy rain obscured the sound of her own paws as they broke the smoothness of the mud. They seemed to be dogs, she thought to herself, but they made no noise. She could not see or hear any humans, and there were no lights on in what appeared to be a house several hundred yards from the cages. All the animals, as she came closer, she was sure were dogs, cowered in the corners of their cages.

She came to the first gate and saw a medium-sized dog. He looked at her suspiciously and then, without speaking, walked a few feet closer. His coat was dull, and he had multiple healing wounds. In some spots, he had no fur; both his ears were torn and mutilated. He had a wide snout with small, yellowish eyes. "What do you want!?" He growled in a barely audible bark.

Casey looked at the other cages. A few dogs were missing ears altogether. One only had one eye, and they all had injuries, some worse than others. One licked a deep gash on his paw that required medical attention. Two of the cages had dogs that were smaller who were curled up in balls, unmoving and afraid and looking with absolute terror at the outside world. "What happened to you?"

Casey whimpered. "What is going on here?"

The dog's eyes darted back and forth, as if he saw not just one animal on the outside, but many. He emitted a menacing growl and bared his teeth. "WHAT DO YOU WANT!?"

She reflexively took a step back. "I...I..."

The dog lunged, losing all control, biting at the cage and barking hysterically. "WHAT DO YOU WANT!? WHAT DO YOU WANT?! WHAT DO YOU WANT?!"

Casey stepped backwards, panting in fright. She heard a faint whimper from a second cage down the line. "He's insane, puppy. Most of them are."

Casey's ears followed the noise to see a hulking short-haired white dog. He was missing a front paw, and he only had one eye. His flank was soaked with blood. "It is difficult to stay sane here."

Casey crouched down near this dog's nose. There was weakness and desperation in his voice. "What has happened here?"

"Fights. Brawls. Whatever they make us do."

Casey instinctively bristled, "But why are you fighting? And who? And why don't the human-mates get help for you?"

The injured hound shifted positions slightly.

Friedwarf whispered in her ear, "You are operating from a perspective that is completely false, dog."

The injured dog continued, "The humans force us to fight other dogs, one another, sometimes a few cats, chickens... really whatever enters their sick, dispassionate minds."

"But why?"

"Dog, we don't know why. Sometimes, the theories are tossed back and forth between some of the newer members. Theories about retribution from past canine lives. Stories about the torture preparing us for a great life beyond this one. Stories about a great canine savior who will come and rescue us. But when the fighting and the beatings continue, we forget about being saved. We only know that we have horribly bad luck and that we hate the humans, the other dogs, the animals around us."

Casey cast a glance back at the first dog, which triggered a threatening growl.

The dog before her anticipated her thoughts, "You see, dog, what happens to more than half of us? Insanity sets in. Usually it starts with pleasurable hallucinations: one dog will whimper about majestic humans clothed in decorative, white large vessels and striking down the abusive ones. The older, weathered and beaten dogs sometimes will shush them or even encourage the fantasies, thinking that it may allay the pain. Finally, the hallucinations transform into vengeful ones: the humans become devils and demons that have been sent to destroy all canines. It's terrible and sad, but those dogs aren't the ones I worry about."

Casey gulped. "Which ones do you worry about?"

"The silent ones. The ones who stare and show no emotion. They become the fiercest to fight, and it becomes the only thing they look forward to. They even come to love our evil captors, and they invariably elevate the humans to the status of deities whilst they become prophets and angels. The complexity of their thinking about our situation is astounding, but they are singular in emotion and action when any animal or thing is thrust in front of them: kill."

Far from the cages, Casey heard stirring in the house. She waited, silent and breathless. Nothing emerged. Casey turned her attention back to the mutilated dog. "I am a senator from the Central Canine Government, and we can liberate you. No canine should be treated as you are. We can free you."

A defeated sigh greeted this declaration. "Senator? Clearly you think your title important, but it will do neither me nor the others any good. Look about you, dog, and you will see that these dogs don't have a familiar look in their eyes. They have no knowledge of loving and nurturing households. I vaguely remember a trace of human kindness from when I was a puppy, before I was dropped off on a distant roadside. There, these humans here picked me up. I thought I was blessed when I was fed and bathed and allowed in a warm house, but only two weeks later, I was thrown into a cage where a dog nearly killed me before I luckily struck a fatal blow. I have a reputation for being lucky while sustaining serious injuries. The humans don't allow us to be cared for because it means their dirty little operation will be closed. Not that it matters: the others could not exist outside of this world. They are unteachable and cannot be rehabilitated. Death is our only liberation. Those that abuse us make us undesirable and unfit for the rest of society. They strike a wound that will never heal. The saddest part of it is that if these wretched humans were killed, these abused dogs and I would weep, because they are also our only source of sustenance and survival. I hate them and wish them death, but their death would likely mean ours as well."

Casey couldn't believe that this was real, and to hear that they refused rescue tore into Casey's heart, and she whimpered pleadingly with the dog. "Well, what can I do? Is there anything we can do?"

"Lead the fananas here."

"How do you know about them? Until a short time ago, they were legends to us."

"Not to us, dog," the canine mused while licking his horribly mangled flank, or at least as far as he could reach along the front of his leg, "they are all too real. Occasionally, the humans will bring an injured one here for the stronger and healthier of us to fight. You see, they have what most of our kind lack: a larger sense of self-awareness. They know the worst of the humans' deeds, and they both fear and loathe them. But we stem from them. The humans selected the weakest and most dependent of the wolves and bred them for their own self-serving desires, and we were the result: a hodge-podge of small and large canines, each structured for specific purposes. Ultimately, the humans look at anything, even when it is working well, and they think 'how could we profit more from this?' Then the fighting rings began. For every human that cuddles and nurtures a puppy, there are twelve that would toss that puppy into a raging river if they could profit off of it. The wolves, however, have no dependence, and though their code is harsh, they know under which circumstances they can dominate the humans. The humans are afraid of them. The injured fanana told me of glorious stories of humans torn apart by packs of them. A month ago, two Yorkies were captured and thrust into our cages as training bait, one in the cage next to mine and he did not last long, the other into my cage—"

"Two Yorkies? Where did they come from?"

"Who knows where any of these humans get any of us? The one dog was lucky he was placed with me. I was horribly injured, even moreso than I am now. My paw had been mangled, and the humans cut it off and burned me at the stump. No dog would willingly fight until his paw had been mangled like that, but this isn't a normal situation. They stand at each end of the cages and give shocks and jolts from sticks. After a while, just them standing there is enough to get us to fight. Better to fight and not get shocked then get shocked and have to fight anyway, after all. Most, especially dogs like Lipper next to me, fight anything placed in there, no matter how big or small, but the humans got distracted by something from the house and they ran off, with just me and the Yorkie in the circle. *I* only fight when I must and for my survival. With them gone, I had little time to act."

"To do what?" Casey was nearly certain that these Yorkies were the ones that had gone missing.

"To help him escape. He tried to talk, but I barked at him to keep quiet and dig. We dug as fast as we could, not knowing when the humans would return, and I told him about this place, about all around us, and why I was helping him. He had a fiery spirit, and when he wriggled under, he lingered to ask me what he could do to help us, all after seeing Lipper maul his brother to death. I told him about the fananas and where they might be found, but that they might kill him on sight. He told me that, one day, he would bring them back. When you came jaunting up here, I half thought you were a fanana. That was a month ago. I sometimes think about him, but then, it doesn't matter anymore, does it?"

Casey jumped out of her skin at the sound of Friedwarf's voice. "My dog friend, we have several scouts near the humans' home. They are signaling to me that the humans will be here soon."

As Casey padded away at the behest of the large rat leader, she barked to the injured dog. "Friend?! Do you know why or how the Yorkies were caught?"

Standing a bit, his strength waning, he replied, "They left, dog. They weren't taken. He told me that he left because he was ignored, ignored for the inventions of the self-absorbed humans."

Friedwarf was practically nipping at Casey's paws to urge her on. A door slammed and human footsteps sounded in the yard. Casey's mind was whirling as she bolted towards the drain. A kernel of thought triggered one final question, "Dog, what was that Yorkie's name that escaped?"

One lone bark as the footsteps closed in. "Fitzy."

As her fat, otter-like yellow tail disappeared into the blackness of the drainage system, she heard human yelling, cages rattling, and awful desperate howling.

SQUIRREL SHORTCUT

Chuckles' legs were burning as he tried to keep pace with the fastest dogs in canine-dom. From time to time, Wicket would bark a brief order at the other dogs, and they would stop, allowing Chuckles to just barely catch up before they lunged forward again. His mind raced with thoughts of Casey's plight and concern for the integrity of the government. Had the Wilds counted on this period of destabilization before making their move, or was it just coincidence? Various policy meetings in months prior had touched upon the possibility that the Wilds had more sophisticated means of garnering intelligence than they did, but, in the end, they could not come to definitive conclusions. Without Casey, he doubted his presence would matter much. He hoped against hope that she was all right.

As they ran, very little of the territory seemed familiar to Chuckles. It stood to reason that the Greyhounds had very specific paths mapped out maximizing speed and convenience. After several hours, the neighborhoods triggered some remote memories from his campaigning.

Curses! Chuckles chastised himself for his betrayal of Casey. Had he not taken that bait from Juniper, Casey may not be stuck in that hole, only to face an indictment at home when she got out. After a time, Chuckles slowed considerably, until Wicket was forced to stop.

"Senator Chuckles," barked the barely panting Greyhound, "I realize it's difficult for you to keep pace, but I must insist you make an effort. We're going to have to go back out when we escort you back to search for Senator Casey. Who knows what kind of trouble she may be in? I have heard some of those areas are rat-infested, not to mention the fananas that may be roaming about."

Chuckles noticed some movement behind Wicket. "I get it, move faster. Where are we now?"

"The new grove where the squirrels generate their report. I doubt they'll mind, they're most definitely resting for the night."

"What makes you so sure? There was something just behind you about a hundred yards down that way," Chuckles made a half-motion casually in that direction. "It was something large, or maybe it just seemed that way given the distance."

Wicket clearly had a sole focus, "It is late, and this grove borders a forest that is not within usual canine-controlled territory." He paused. "We should keep moving. We are built for speed, not protection."

The grove was unusually silent. Again, he saw motion, but this time, he could have sworn there were several animals moving about. "This is supposed to be neutral territory," Chuckles said. "The squirrels leave acorns inscribed with warnings around the perimeter. They only tolerate us during particular hours. Other than the birds, there should be no other creatures here." Chuckles trotted towards the animals.

"Senator, we simply do not have time for this!"

Chuckles turned. "Do I outrank you? Are you going to be so bold as to defy a direct order from me? Is it my size that makes you think you can do so?" Chuckles seemed to be hovering above the ground; he was barking so hard.

"N-n-no, of course not, Senator," Wicket stammered. He then looked back nervously at his two aides and briefly barked for them to continue to advance. He would stay back with Chuckles and personally ensure his safety.

Plowing forward, Chuckles was twenty yards towards the far end of the squirrels' grove before he heard a warning yip. Wicket charged up to accompany him. There were three different creatures: two were small and looked like squirrels, but the third looked like a dog, and a large one at that. Chuckles was suddenly grateful that Wicket was there, and almost wished he had the extra insurance of the other two.

Chuckles padded closer, and the trio froze. The large dog-like creature bolted off into the woods, and one of the small animals headed right for them. Even with the darkness, Chuckles could see that it wasn't a squirrel.

"Rocko?!?"

"Ohhhh, Senator Chuckles, fancy seeing you here. I was uh- just talking over some matters with the head squirrel about the report for tomorrow. You know, giving some details about today's dealings to make sure the report is complete and such." The gopher either appeared nervous or Chuckles had not seen enough gophers to determine their state of mind.

"The Squirrel Report is generated each morning from scentimas carried from insects from each corner of our territory. The squirrels do not respond to any information carried directly by us, or by any other animal."

"W-w-well, you know, Senator, sir, times are w-w-well, changing. They actually specifically requested me to give them the details of our current meeting. T-t-those crazy squirrels, guess they remain quite the mystery." Do gophers sweat, Chuckles was wondering?

Chuckles looked past Rocko but could not make out either figure that had been there previously. "Really…," Chuckles growled back.

Rocko scratched his head. "Umm, well, actually you know what it was, Senator? The lead squirrel was just clarifying some points from today because there was an interruption in the insect traffic because of the weather and all. I was just helping to ensure that it wouldn't happen again."

"Why don't you call your little friend there, maybe I'll ask him some questions. Or maybe you'd rather speak to the Bulldog Police?" Chuckles advanced to within centimeters of Rocko. He could almost smell the lie.

"Well, you know, he's so tired, long day and all," Rocko spat out.

"Call him!"

"Senator! He is a very busy squirrel, and this would not be an orthodox approach, perhaps if I walk back with you to see Senator Juniper we can—"

"CALL HIM!!" Chuckles bared enough teeth to get the message across that he was willing to use more than just the force of his words.

Rocko dashed a glance in the direction of the dog park as if Juniper himself was going to bound out of the woods to defend him. Where the trio had been meeting, he made a series of taps on the tree followed by some barely audible clicks.

A few minutes passed before the lead squirrel poked his head out of a hovel and angrily clicked at Rocko. Rocko responded with a few more clicks of his own, and the squirrel first withdrew his head only to come winding down the tree from another hole not within Chuckles' sight. He lazily came up to Chuckles and Wicket with Rocko in tow.

"Well, Senator, what would you like to ask him? I can handily translate for you."

"Ask him who the other creature was that you were meeting with?"

A series of clicks and exchanges all the while the squirrel would only occasionally meet Chuckles' stares.

"He says he is not sure what you are referring to and he thinks that with such darkness you are likely mistaken. It was just he and myself." If a gopher could be smug, Rocko certainly met the task.

Chuckles stared at the rodent duo. Wicket stood with his back to the group, as if on watch, but he was uneasy and whimpered urgency. Chuckles resorted to a different tactic.

"Rocko, ask him how the Squirrel Report went today, ask him if there were any aberrations."

Rocko relayed Chuckles' message in a series of clicks and noises. The lead squirrel was surprisingly brief in response. Rocko turned back to Chuckles, "He says this is not the time to go through such nonsense, the report is what it is. He is tired and wants to go to bed."

Chuckles turned to Wicket, "Let's go. I don't know what's going on here, but this squirrel isn't forthcoming. A shame if the Wilds end up invading; we'll see how sympathetic they are to these temperamental reporters."

"Neither of them are telling you the truth!" A lone voice shot out from the darkness on the east edge of the grove towards the dog park. The party of four was located on the western edge.

Rocko froze. Chuckles looked at him first, half-expecting Rocko to own up to this voice of dissension, but Rocko was paralyzed, although he seemed to want to run. Wicket noticed the source first, "It's a black dog coming at us, smallish about medium-sized, mixed-breed, longish hair." Chuckles assumed that Wicket's keen vision accompanied his tremendous speed, as he could barely make out the galloping figure. Height, speed, and great vision—some dogs are blessed with good lines, Chuckles thought to himself.

Bruno sauntered up. Chuckles noticed he seemed never to be in a rush, although the tone of his voice suggested grave concern. "He's lying, Senator Chuckles, the gopher isn't saying what he's telling you: the squirrel is cursing at you."

Chuckles' anger welled up into a deep, throaty growl, and when he turned, Rocko was backpedaling. "Who you gonna believe, Senator Chuckles, a former hospital inmate? He's just making things up, he doesn't speak squirrel." The lead squirrel was ignoring the lot of them and was making his way back to the tree. "Besides," Rocko continued, "what a squirrel says doesn't matter anyway."

"Except for the fact that we depend on these squirrels for information. We interpret the reports designated to us, but we've been fools not to question the sources of these reports. You, Rocko, stay right there and you…you…squirrel, STOP!"

Bruno let fly with a series of clicks, and the squirrel shot back in kind and leapt up to a spot halfway up the tree. Rocko himself backing up, Wicket was completely oriented in the opposite direction, and Chuckles was hopping from one side to another barking at the two to stay put when Bruno exploded from a standstill, brusquely grabbed the squirrel around his midsection, and flung him to the ground. Before the squirrel could recover, Bruno had a firm paw on its neck. The desperate animal flashed some teeth and claws, but Bruno gave him a warning growl and pressed a bit harder, demonstrating his superior strength and position. Chuckles raced up and hissed a growl in the lead squirrel's ear for added measure.

"Alright Bruno," Chuckles relished this opportunity, "ask him who he and the gopher were with."

Obliging, and with some chatter, there was a little bit of back and forth before Bruno barked the answer. His paw, snout and gaze stayed focused on the squirrel.

"He says a fanana."

This also succeeded in getting the attention of Wicket, who chimed in quickly before Chuckles could generate a response, "Senator, if that's true, then we desperately need to get you back to the dog park to convene with the rest of the Congress. We could be in a deeper crisis than we thought!"

Although usually excitable, Chuckles gathered himself without panic. "Easy, Wicket, we've been here awhile already; they could have easily overwhelmed us if they wanted to. The fanana likely retreated back to the main group, which is probably far from here." Chuckles spoke so confidently, he half-convinced himself that this was the truth. Reassured but agitated, Wicket made some short paces before settling down again. Chuckles gritted his jaws at the squirrel, "Ask this arrogant thing why, Bruno."

An exchange. "He says that the squirrels are the main source of media, and that they do not have to explain their actions to any of us."

What gall! Chuckles was impressed at the squirrel's gumption, defying them even with a paw pressing on his neck. "Don't they know how dangerous the fananas are? Don't they know that they have no code of ethics or morals? That they kill for their own satisfaction?"

After the relay, Bruno replied, "He says that even if we don't understand their guiding principles, that does not mean they don't have them. He says their anger is just a reflection of how they have been marginalized all these years, while we have enjoyed the opulence of living near the humans."

"I don't believe this." Chuckles was stunned—all the decisions they had made based on the Squirrel Reports!

Bruno continued to translate, the squirrel was on a roll, "We are the voice of all animals, not just the canines, and we report the information in an unbiased filter. To spread the messages of your political parties without hearing from a side that has no voice, we would do a disservice to those that depend upon us."

"How long and how much information is filtered through your fanana friends?"

The squirrel paused a minute. Bruno growled and repeated the question. Finally, a halting response, "He claims that he's not sure what you mean and reiterates that they are not under anyone's paw of influence, but rather seek to deliver the stories that are otherwise ignored. He says there are stories of sadness, and famine, and oppressive humans, and if we did not have such an intertwined relationship with them, we might see these faults for ourselves."

Chuckles swiped a glance at Wicket, who gave him another pleading whine. "Tell him we get it. The squirrel media spreads messages of hate in the name of honesty in reporting, but, make no mistake, when the fananas take over, squirrels may be their first meal. Let's go, Bruno. Our government may be facing its last crisis before it ceases to resemble a government."

Before Bruno could leave, the squirrel spewed some more chatter. Bruno, Chuckles, and Wicket were halfway to the other side of the grove. "Do you want to know what he said, sir?" Bruno barked.

"I think we've listened to the squirrels long enough."

After they left, a small Italian Greyhound, watching from the forest, spat in anger. A fanana breathed into his ear, "We've come too far to fail, Early."

"Bring ten of your finest warriors. Enough of this finesse. All animals die when you cut off their heads. We'll need to strike at the epicenter of the Central Canine Government." The fanana laughed and bounded away.

IN LEAGUE TO LIBERATE

Soaked and shivering, Casey was bent on return as she navigated the tunnels. They walked in thick, angry silence. Friedwarf knew that canines were more sensitive than rats to the harming of their own kind. He turned some thoughts over in his mind before thinking that Casey might think the rats were connected to this. "Dog," he said, "we have no means to free your caged friends."

No response.

"I never heard of this Fitzy before, but we would be happy to help you locate him if you think it would help."

Again, no response. Friedwarf thought that maybe his Domesticated Common was not as fluent as he had remembered. "Dog, do you—"

"I heard you," Casey snapped. "We've been so dependent on the humans that we did not realize the extent of our own dependency. I would have never considered that they could be the source of such betrayal. It's something that takes more than just the few minutes to absorb, so you'll excuse me."

"We rats are used to our own extermination. It's sad, but we have the weight of numbers. These kinds of things strengthen our resolve, but in different, less tangible ways. We redirect, we look for other angles. That's why I'm optimistic that a valid historical record will free us from this cycle."

Casey plodded on, barking with a melancholy tone, "I am trying to see how we could have been so wrong in assuming that we shared something with the humans. Our entire governmental system has been a sham. I wouldn't know where to start tearing it down because it runs so seamlessly with human existence."

His whiskers flickered, "If I may, dog, offer some thoughts given our historical perspective?"

An unenthusiastic yip, "Go ahead."

"Well," Friedwarf said, "we've noticed that the humans truly have built large civilizations over time, but there is also some who argue that other trends can be found within the greater picture. What do all animals share?"

As they turned down yet another dank, dark corridor, Casey's patience waned, "I don't know, we're all alive at some point?"

"Exactly, dog, the life cycle. We are born and are young and mature over time. We reach a peak point of prominence within our groups or clans or herds, and then we decline, some more quickly than others, unless misfortune strikes us down sooner, and then we die. Others take our place, either literally or figuratively. The humans, on massive levels, appear to have some cycles that may get more elaborate over time, but still repeat with striking and sometimes very predictable regularity."

"Do we have much farther?" she whined, although she secretly thought it was an interesting premise. To think that a few weeks prior these brilliant historians would have been disregarded as just nameless vermin!

"Just a few more turns and we'll have you on your way. We teach such a proposition to our prospective historians in simpler terms. When they live alone, it fails, then they move to groups, that fails, they swing back to alone, but they change a thing or two things, and then back to groups, and so on."

"So?" Casey retorted.

"So, you are thinking about tearing down your government. We can say with only a few exceptions that the human civilizations that abandon things abruptly often fail, but the resilient ones tweak things a tad."

"How could we not cut the ties with humans when we see how little they value us? Those dogs were dying back there! They were desperate and had no hope left, but if I ignore them, then I am just as guilty of harming them and future other dogs as the wretched humans that are abusing them now."

"No doubt there must be changes, dog, but you are likely to achieve more success if you have a fallback system. Ahhh, here we are. See the moonlight? You're only a few neighborhoods from your own and the dog park." The tunnel opened, revealing a chilly, brisk night, with the trickle of water coming from a small stream. It was another storm drain. Outside, a small park where humans often played. Casey knew this park well and recognized the location.

"Fallback system?"

"Huria, Senator, would be your perfect alternative." A lean, muscled Madison offered with a smart bark. The bedraggled Asher and Peachtree were at her side, accompanied by another dozen or so various other dogs, all mixed breeds.

"It's not a setup, Senator," Friedwarf said soothingly. "We were asked by the ever reliable Madison here, a local leader, I guess you could say governor of several blocks in the city, to help them out to intervene nonviolently with the Central Canine Government. It was not our aim to approach you, but you arrived at an opportune time. I think you should hear Madison out."

Before Casey could venture a whimper, the bold Madison approached her and deferentially started, "Senator, I knew it was you because we have a far more vast network supplying us information. Scentimas, to be sure, are important, but we also contract with various feline agencies and several mice and rat networks. For months now, we have appreciated a growing discontent within your government, and now you have seen firsthand the true nature of the humans. Most of us are undocumented former human companions, and we all left for a myriad of reasons. We govern at a local level, and we network with one another mainly for protection of our way of life and to ensure that the specific rights of each of our canines are not compromised. Your government has become too big and unwieldy, Senator, and if it implodes without any support, there will be chaos. I assure you that we are not in league with the fananas. There is only one problem: I am one of only a few that would like a peaceful solution. We have more than twenty governors and only three, maybe four, of us have nonviolent intentions. We are approaching canines in each neighborhood for support for a peaceful transition with the promise that their huria will be our primary goal at all times. Our message brings no threat, and we are only sending out small groups. The vast majority of governors, however, have been conditioned to hate and loathe the Central Canine Government, and it will only take a small amount of resistance in one area to set off a violent coup of your government. Your Bulldogs and Rat Terriers are tough, and we know you have considerable forces at your disposal, but we outnumber you four to one. I need your help, and you need ours. You are a well respected and prestigious senator, and the weight of your bark suggesting a unification of our two governments would go a long way towards making canine lives better for all."

Casey's fur stood on end, but she reeled it back in with a guided bark, "Then what? We succumb to your ways and the idea of some benefitting for the sake of a few, while canines are left to their own devices? Look at your own numbers: there is not a small toy breed member among you. The human-mates have a place for them, but there is not such a role for them in the streets."

"You have seen the dogs in the cages, you have seen what the humans are capable of, Senator."

Casey responded feverishly and ferociously. "You know of them?! So why are they still there, why have you not come to their aid with all of your superior forces?"

Madison was cool and calm. "We have, Senator Casey. Many times. They have been so conditioned that they cannot be re-trained. They are violent, sociopathic, unpredictable. A few lived sheltered lives for a few years before being captured by the local pound and had a tendency towards meanness, and most are downright dangerous. When humans abuse those that have less, the damage is often irreparable. The wounds heal, the *physical* injuries fade, but the savage demeanors of those that we saved were evidence of the *true* damage of the human touch."

"So what will become of them?" Casey could feel her heart racing as if she was experiencing the horror of their fate herself.

"Nothing can be done. We avoid the area as if it's been cursed by some unknown, ancient religion. Even with our numbers, to attack the humans would be suicide and would ignite a vengeful backlash in all of our neighborhoods."

Casey did not respond, but instead nosed her way past Madison and her cohorts. Asher and Peachtree cast confused glances at Madison, who tilted her head in an equally perplexed manner.

Casey padded towards the dog park with the earnestness of a sled dog. She was clearly a leader among followers. "Senator," Madison barked, "where are you going, and do you want us to follow?"

"If you want to truly liberate the canines, then you have to confront the government first."

Madison tore after her, and Asher brought up the rear. "Madison," she hissed, "this is not going according to plan."

"By all accounts, Casey is no fool, Asher. I don't think there is any dog more apt to incite a positive change than her, especially one that has witnessed the dogs in the cages."

"But we don't really know her!"

"Without her, there is only violence. Trusting this dog is the best thing I can do for the dogs that rely on me."

Asher angrily persisted, "But how do you know?!"

"I don't."

CONFRONTATION

"All the votes have been cast," a chipper Juniper proclaimed. "Clearly they reflect the fact that Casey has been in league with the enemy. She is hereby purged from this Congress, and her committee votes bear no more weight. I would say this is a victory not only for bipartisan canine politics, but for all canine-dom. In addition, let me further add that I have a contingency plan that accounts for this invasion by the Wilds. If it is war they want, then war they shall have."

Sasha, ashamed and surrounded by a Bulldog escort, was relegated to observing the remainder of the proceedings. She felt in the depth of her heart that this would be the ultimate end of the Central Canine Government. She did not know the numbers of the Wilds slowly squeezing the life out of the government, but she knew they outnumbered them substantially. She sighed to herself, wondering how only a few short weeks ago the government had seemed so stable. Now, it was clear that staving off full-on control by the Wilds, one way or another, was impossible. All any of them ever did was talk. The Beagle continued to rally support with ears all turned towards him. Even President Darma seemed to take a back seat to the powerful Juniper.

"You see, it is as I've been barking all along. We should have been more proactive. We should not have rested on our haunches, performing tricks and taking treats from humans. The Contrarian party is appropriately named, because what the party has fed to its constituents is exactly contrary to what we should have done. Now, we appear to be in a dire place, and though we have had disagreements, the Dominance match between myself and the President has settled the matter. The votes of Casey's committee members have been rightly discounted.[19] Now, with the Wilds coming down on us, the only solution is war."

---

19 There is little available record to explain the outcome of the Dominance matches and what it had to do with the subsequent voting. Some historians claim that Juniper and the Bulldogs enacted a military coup that later fell apart due to events following. Others contend that it was explained by various lost arcane laws that allowed for Juniper to disallow an entire committee's votes.

"Yet, all the scentima reports show that no violence whatsoever has been committed by the Wilds, and that several neighborhoods have simply peacefully given in to them," barked a junior senator dog from the Health Committee.

"Ha! So far, all I have stated has occurred exactly as I have predicted. You fools, it's a ruse to draw us out. Once we leave this dog park, the Wilds will not hesitate to violently dispatch us. Without representation, without governmental guidance, who else do the laydogs have to turn to?"

"How can you be sure that that is what they are planning to do?"

"Because it's what *I* would do," Juniper arrogantly barked back at the dissenting voice. "The government is in crisis now, fellow canine Senators and Representatives. We need to be equally bold and extreme in the direction that we take. The government is being overrun by the Wilds, but I have secret reserve forces ready to turn this conflict away from us, but more, I bark, more must be done."

Silence now. Juniper continued with renewed confidence that a landslide would ratify his proposal. The fear of loss of their offices was the prime motivator, and he knew that, regardless of party, fear trumped all others.

"I have the forces to stop this invasion, I promise you that. Yet, we need to emerge from this crisis even stronger."

"How do you propose to do that?"

Juniper seemed to be smiling, "We should call for Section thirteen to be enacted. If the majority of districts give a vote of no-confidence, then President Darma, who has run us into this crisis, is removed and leadership goes to myself and the committee heads of the Committees of Health and Human Endearment. With us in control, and with all of my resources at my disposal, I can avoid the messy bureaucracy usually required to strengthen our fighting forces. You will finally see how beautifully efficient we can make this government. Dogs will feel safer and more secure."

"But how will we avoid another Big Cull?"

Silence again. Even Sasha was impressed by the depth of Juniper's plan, loathsome as she found him to be. There was uneasiness in the dog park, and the senators and representatives looked about nervously. President Darma sat in the back, stoic, and completely silenced.

"The Wilds are invading now. Dogs are likely dying now. Another Big Cull may be the price of our freedom. We need to be more concerned about having solid leadership in place once the bodies of this war start to cool."

A lone severe bark chimed in from the most southern corner of the dog park, "I have a question first." The entire Congress, familiar with the sound of the bark, turned to see Senator Casey with several strange cats and dogs in tow.

Juniper smiled, baring his teeth, and barked coolly back, "Senator! You're just in time to be arrested for treason. The Bulldog Police will, I am sure, be happy to take you and whomever you have with you into custody."

"They're members of the Wilds," she growled and barreled her way into the center circle.

An array of barks and growls erupted from the conclave of dogs. Never before had any members of the Wilds set foot in the dog park. Cries of "traitor" were heard over the ruckus. The Bulldogs looked a bit restless as they stood ground, trying to maintain order.

"I never thought you would be so deliberately foolish as to bring your co-conspirators in with you, Senator Casey. You may not have realized it, but I have already shown, with the help of several eye witnesses, how you have undermined this government." The throe of dogs seemed to want to tear Casey and Madison and her crew to pieces. Asher defensively eyed a few dogs nearest to her that she decided she would target first should a melee occur. The Bulldogs were especially keen on Asher and other felines in the group, knowing they would likely need to take their ferocity into account should violence erupt.

"Senators and Representatives, these dogs and cats are members of the Wilds. They approached me to aid them in a non-violent, peaceful coup of our government." Casey let the last remnant of the phrase sink in with her canine audience before continuing.

"Before I entered, I heard Juniper's plan. With the fananas and the Wilds at the gate, Juniper would have you believe that trusting in our system will save us all…with himself at the helm, of course. What he is not telling you is that, if he is successful in turning back the Wilds, then he has no plan for keeping us endeared to the humans. If a tri-dogverate is in place, it won't be long before Juniper co-opts control from the other two, leaving a president that was never elected. He *wants* this chaos! He's planned for this, counting on any governmental crisis during which he could say that as long as we trust in him, then he can carry us through."

"Ha, again with our human-mates!" Juniper growled. "Now is the time for action, canine action! How could you listen to this treasonous dog, who brings the Wilds with her!?"

Casey responded, barking over the little Beagle, "The humans have helped our numbers grow. That, I cannot deny. Yet, they are a double-edged beast, like a porcupine, like a skunk, so nice to be around or to see, but with an evil, terrible secret."

Only occasional pants could be heard. Even the Bulldogs had paused in their attempt to arrest Casey. The severity of her rhetoric had all the dogs captivated.

Juniper ran at and around the stalwart Casey, who stood frozen like a statue, and barked in the snouts of the Bulldogs and Rat Terrier security forces, "Don't you see? She's a traitor! Don't you see she comes with our enemy?! Don't give her a pulpit to spout her ridiculous theories. She and Lucky were in *league*, they met in private discussing plans to *overthrow* all of you so that she could take power for herself with the Wilds as her personal army!"

Dozens of canine snouts quickly shifted focus from Juniper to Casey. Juniper's loyalty, his notion of carambee, was never in question. Although quieter, Casey was regarded just as highly. She was a silent, strong, and brilliant senator.

"Listen," Casey barked back, "there is so much we never knew. Our first assumption of the generosity, love, and devotion of humans to us is only the first in many lies. Yes, I met with Lucky, only to find he was radicalized, convinced that the only response to the fananas that threatened his West-town culture was to get more extreme and rely on roof rats!"

Murmurs of surprise echoed across the dog park.

Casey continued, "Yes, disgusting, abhorrent, and that is exactly what I thought when he sought to trap me and dispose of me to advance his traitorous agenda. And in getting back, I found refuge with noble and wonderful creatures—Norway rats. They showed me the history, the written account of events that we could never keep track of. The humans have advanced; they have built and invented *things* that they have used to craft their world as they see fit. Now, we are in danger of becoming a useless afterthought to those same things to which they attribute so much value. Their objects, houses, and toys have become their source of attention and distraction while we ... fetch things for them. Companionship!? Devotion?! Carambee!?? The humans know *nothing* of these things, not in the way that we all know and value them."

Juniper interjected a bark, "Senator Casey, I have never in all my years heard of such—"

"They're not theories! I have seen proof of the treachery of our reliance on humans, proof of the malice that they are capable of when they cease to regard us as highly as we regard them!!" Casey was viciously barking at Juniper. They both stood with hair puffed out. The rhetoric of Casey's speech had finally sunk in and ignited a hellish chorus from the senators and representatives. As the dogs barked at one another, they reflexively divided into multiple partisan groups. The frenzy threatened to disintegrate further when a scared yelp caught the attention of all.

A bloodied Cocker Spaniel was crying at the edge of the fence looking in on the meeting area, "I am from North-town ... the fananas have come in outrageous numbers. They have routed us all. Any that stayed were run down, savaged terribly. I barely escaped ..."

The dog collapsed, likely exhausted from the trek to deliver the message.

Chaos and panic started to set in. At that time, a low buzz could be heard from around the dog park from all directions. Not thunder, but still menacing, some of the smaller representatives swore that the ground was vibrating.

Juniper saw his chance. "The *other* party, those Contrarians have given all of us promises that they could not fulfill. This is a time of crisis!!" Saliva flew from his mouth as he barked savagely. "Only a strong leader, with the government at his back, could bring us the kind of stability that this government needs! The fananas attack as a *result* of the failed policies of President Darma and her do-nothing senators!"

The pitch of the buzz jumped an octave. Although the wind swirled in the distance, it died within the confines of the dog park. Scattered barks in fear peppered the group of senators and representatives, but Juniper still overpowered them.

"Look at this dog! A concrete example of the failed policies of President Darma and her corrupt senators!"

"Madison!" Division, the once proud German Shepherd mix, limped up to the fence separating the dog park from the outside world. "We were ambushed, Madison. Even as I had designs to force the citizens. We were torn apart before we could ever get to our target. Dozens of the fananas! They struck so swiftly and silently. I'm all that's left."

Anxiety welled up inside Madison as she placed a paw on the fence near Division's face. "Division! What about Orchard?"

Division's breathing was labored. "I don't know if he's ok...I just ran, the fananas are bloodthirsty." He sunk silently.

The blare of the buzz persisted. Undeniable, Madison backed away from the fence and whispered to Casey, "What is that?"

Casey gulped, "I don't know."

Juniper still dominated as he sensed the growing fear, "I have warned all of you! I predicted this downfall. I fought and labored, and now it is nearly too late—*nearly*!!! WE MUST IMMEDIATELY PASS A SECTION THIRTEEN!! GIVE ME THE POWER TO BRING US BACK FROM THE BRINK!"

A few of the representatives started to bark support. But others screamed, "You wanted to offer the fananas citizenship! They are tearing up our neighborhoods!"

Now rising to a deafening level, the buzz nearly suffocated all random barks and whimpers. Only Juniper could be heard as he pressed his advantage further. Despite the fear of the fananas, he was strong and confident.

"NOW, MY FELLOW PUPS, JOIN ME TO OUST CASEY AND HER LIES, AND TOGETHER WE WILL FACE THIS NEW CHALLENGE. THE FANANAS WILL RESPECT OUR STRENGTH, OUR NEWFOUND SOLIDARITY. IT'S THE WEAKNESS OF YOUR CONTRARIAN PRESIDENT THAT ALLOWED THIS TO HAPPEN!"

And then it happened. Darkness. A mass of bees, gnats, flies, wasps simultaneously descended upon the Central Canine Congress and President.

For minutes, the sound of their wings smothered all dialogue like a chainsaw. However loud the sound, it was the scentimas. Hundreds of thousands of snippets of information initially over-whelmed the panicking Congress. All of the scentimas painted the vivid, horrific portrait of the tortured dogs that lay dying every day in the cages. The gore. The cruelty of the humans. The entire history of all the dogs that died dumped into the Congress' con-sciousness. Like a continuous awful loop playing on their deepest fears, the mass of insects infected the dogs again and again, dump-ing scentima upon scentima. In only a few minutes, the catharsis of the insects finished. En masse, they lifted. The moonlight once again lit the proceedings.

Most of the senators and representatives were crying and whim-pering. Others were angry. The silence pulsed like a heartbeat.

Casey seized the moment. "Juniper talks of these strategies to keep us safe, but they are all built on the lies that we can trust the humans. Now you know it is not so. You can fight the Wilds, but then you continue to live a lie."

"What do we do?" One dog barked. "We are not fit to live in the outdoors. Many of the smaller breeds cannot survive on the streets."

"We give all those we rule over a choice. We are faced with a great crisis that touches upon our fundamental way of living. We offer each district the opportunity to take part in our government, with an eye on the humans and their destructive tendencies. We operate in league with the humans, but reserve the right to abandon them at any moment. We give those in the Wilds equal status. The concept of huria means that dogs can choose how they want to live, how much government they want to enjoy, and how much humans they want in their lives. With a joint government, freely elected by all canines that keeps canine interests in mind with the knowledge of the true nature of humans, maybe then we can enjoy true security."

"This is outrageous!" Juniper screamed. "It will be chaos!"

A tiny voice responded loudly, "I will show you chaos!" Early stood at the entrance to the dog park.

Juniper cocked his head, "Early? What are you talking about? Get over here!"

"No. I have listened to you for long enough." Several of the senators, despite the gravity of the situation, laughed at the little aide.

"You laugh, huh?" Early ran around nipping at their faces as he barked. "You've all been played. Juniper *planned* the whole lot of this. Your fear, the lack of information … he specifically directed us to block key scentimas about intelligence so that any threats could go unnoticed." Early smugly looked at Juniper.

Gasps and whispering. Juniper started to back towards the entrance, "What a ridiculous notion! I am a distinguished member—"

"He *knew* he could count on the fear to force a vote for the tri-dogverate. Once he had that in place, it was only a matter of time before Juniper dispatched his co-leaders."

Juniper showed a glint of teeth and started to march towards Early.

"You're all fools! Which is why I sought real power. Animals that could keep the order in all sorts of times." Juniper was almost on top of Early, and then he lunged.

"Juniper watch out!" Casey had seen the massive grey fanana come from the side and knocked Juniper out of the air with its paws. Juniper tumbled a dozen feet and lay whimpering. Framing Early, ten wolves growling and drooling advanced. Although there were dozens of dogs, most had never seen a fight, and the vicious beasts licked their lips. They were going to enjoy eliminating the whole of the Central Canine Government. Early was laughing until Madison let loose a lusty howl.

"Hooooooooowwwwwwwwwwwwwllllllllllll!!!!!!!!"

A switch flipped, and Asher, Peachtree and the other Wilds members turned into snarling masses ready to fight.

Early laughed. "Oh, Casey, you come with a few of the Wilds and think you can take on one of nature's perfect fighting machines? Ha! Once we get in power, *our* way of life, *our* religion will be the law! The law of the fananas!!!" The wolves laughed maniacally in support.

"Oh, Early, you have miscalculated a bit," Casey barked a series of three barks in accordance with a second howl from Madison.

Street-hardened, battle-tested dozens of members of the Wilds with EastandMain, the tough Boxer leader, exploded out of the forest, peppered with dozens more of the Bulldog Police. The wolves turned to the greater threat, and the rescue force quickly disposed of a couple near the edge.

"There'll be more!!" Early screeched.

EastandMain laughed, "No more, little puppy, at least around here. We lost contact with Division's group when they ran ahead, but we re-established order in all areas after a rendezvous with Senator Casey and Madison before cleaning up the rest of your little coup. With our forces united, the fananas didn't stand a chance."

The Bulldog Police came up to usher Early, Juniper, and the rest of the fananas away. The Central Canine Congress breathed a collective sigh.

Barks of "Casey for President!!" greeted Madison, Casey, and President Darma as they sent out several Greyhounds to signal that all was well with the government.

A truce was called with the Wilds and the CCG. Whispers of a new creed encompassing the ideals of huria and carambee started to unfold. Madison mused, "It will be a mess for a while, Senator Casey."

"Maybe contentious for a time," Casey half-agreed, "but necessary. And there is one other important note. We must have consensus on the basic rights of dogs, rights that one Yorkie named

Fitzy felt were being threatened. Fitzy left in search of the fananas because he thought that only extremism could solve his problems. The fananas, the wolves, adhere to absolute truths. It was that absoluteness that Fitzy was attracted to. We have failed not only Fitzy, but all dogs that are abused at the hands of humans."

"The fananas' culture is different, and you make it sound barbaric because it is foreign. Their notions are different than ours, but, like us, they want to survive," barked another member of Juniper's committee.

"Lies," barked Chuckles, who had padded in shortly after Juniper was led off with Early, "lies propagated by the Squirrel Report, the media on which we rely. The lead squirrel himself took information from the fananas themselves. The fananas used them as a mouthpiece to throw us all into disarray."

Casey gazed favorably at Chuckles and Bruno. "The squirrels ignore that the fananas committed real harms. They live near West-town and oppose the West-town culture in favor of some kind of zealotry that borders on barbarism and despotism."

"So, what do we do about them?" another junior representative quipped. "Sure we have quelled a rebellion now, but ... ?"

"I think that Madison and EastandMain will find a union with our forces to be very helpful in ensuring our safety," Casey barked in response. Madison stayed behind with Casey as EastandMain and the head of the Bulldog Police trotted off to compare notes about the remainder of the fananas and their movements. The remnants of Juniper's defense staff lagged behind to offer further assistance. Simultaneously, President Darma started to receive some scentimic status reports.

"So, Senator Labrador-Casey, what's next?" Sasha piped up.

"We vote on passage of S.B. 3629, which I have dubbed The Fitzy Resolution."

The vote, after brief debates about the precise wording of the bill, took place and was ratified by a two-thirds majority in the Senate and nearly sixty percent support in the House.

The Fitzy Resolution

→ Each dog and living thing that lives at the mercy of others shall have the right, to which no one can obviate, to rise up to those that seek to oppress it.

→ Each dog and living thing that lives at the mercy of others shall have the right to safety and happiness.

→ Each dog and living thing that lives at the mercy of others shall have the right to share its huria with those that he or she sees fit.

→ Each dog and living thing that lives at the mercy of others has the right to live with or without government.

→ Each dog that lives at the mercy of others has an equal vote towards the government as any other dog.

→ Each dog and living thing that lives at the mercy of others is always and undeniably free no matter the circumstances.

→ Any being, human or otherwise, that harms dogs or living things that depend upon them, either through direct action or neglect, is deemed cursed and hateful for all eternity.

After the vote, Casey left the dog park, uneasy about the future. Many canines would leave the humans, regardless of any infraction, as was now their right. It was dark now, and the leaves were falling from the trees on a windy, moonlight-filled night. As she exited one corner of the dog park, a field lay before her. A smallish figure stood about fifty yards in front of her. She paused, and it appeared to be looking at her, too. It looked like a Yorkshire Terrier. Casey bolted, and it took off into a nearby cover of trees. She barked just before it disappeared, "Fitzy!"

The figure paused. It started to take off again.

Casey barked again, "Fitzy! You can come back!"

The figure paused again but did not turn, and it disappeared into the woods.

"But what will you do?!" Casey barked again. There was no answer.

As Casey went home, she noticed there was a general exodus of dogs from their owners. There was going to be a period of general unrest in the canine world, Casey thought to herself. She had not made up her mind whether she would return to her own humans. When she neared the driveway of her home, a gnat buzzed by with a status update. The Bulldog Police, with the aid of the Wilds, had bolstered defenses around most areas. The wolves were not strong enough in number to combat the might of the combined forces. EastandMain had also, calculatingly, left the fields near the abused dogs completely undefended. Casey sighed sadly. Should she go home?

A door at the back of Casey's home opened, and a human female voice shouted, "Caaaaaaasssseeeey?"

She paused for a second and bolted in its direction. She loved her humans. She was one of the lucky ones, and she knew it.

🐾

The men that tended the cages stomped out to feed the dogs. They did not notice that their guns, knives, and even tools were missing. It was dark. As they clustered around the cages, they heard a sound. Many, many wolves' eyes glared from the darkness around them. Throaty growls sounded, and with a single bark, they fell on them. If one listened closely, an angry Yorkie could be heard in the din.

THE END